KNOCKING BOOTS

JORDAN MARIE

KNOCKING Boots

Lucas Brothers Book 5

By:

Jordan Marie

**I've always heard, don't fall in love with a cowboy.
I should have listened.**

I've sworn off men.
They've never given me much in life, except a bun in the oven
and grief.
My kids are my life and all that truly matter.

Until him.

Jansen Reed is a living fantasy straight from the old west.
Sexy drawl, tight jeans and that glint in his eyes that makes my
knees weak.
He promises me the ride of my life.
And serves it up—on the kitchen table.

Something about Jansen makes me want to believe in fairytales
again.
But, I'm not the kind of girl who gets a happy ending.
Never have been.
There will come a day when my cowboy will ride away, leaving
me shattered.
I've accepted it and eventually I'll make him realize it, too.
Too bad I can't convince my kids….

**You thought you knew this family, but boy are you in
for a surprise. Travel back in time with the Lucas
family and discover that these kids are just like their
mother when it comes to matchmaking.**
*Can be read as a complete standalone book. Happy
Ever After guaranteed.*

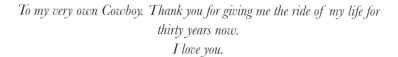

To my very own Cowboy. Thank you for giving me the ride of my life for thirty years now.
I love you.

Foreword

I know you guys who have followed this series were anxious for Blue and Meadow's story. I started it, but that story is a little emotional and after writing Rory, I needed a break. I've been suffering a bit of writer's block and slowly Ida Sue began talking. Her story wasn't what I was expecting. When I first wrote the other books, Ida Sue was comic relief for me. Now, she's real. I want to hug her and spend time with her and don't tell my husband, but I want a Jansen of my very own.

This book was a bear to write. I had to align all the ages, timelines, etc. I drove my girls crazy working it all out. I did some updating on The Perfect Stroke, because Gray thought in it that his mother and Jansen had a free and open relationship. I soon discovered that was not what Jansen and Ida Sue wanted—and Jansen wouldn't let it happy at all. He's very territorial.

I hope you guys enjoy the story. As always, I'd love if you reach out to me and let me know! I love hearing from you guys. My links and contact info is in the back.

Xoxo

J

```
┌─────────────────────────────┐
│                             │
│             1               │
│                             │
│          Jansen             │
│                             │
└─────────────────────────────┘
```

"YOU'RE NEW TO THESE PARTS."

I look up to see a man close to my own age walk out of the store front where I'm standing.

"Yeah. Just got here today." I lean up against the post, light up my cigarette and let my eyes wander again to the woman standing ten feet away from me. She has a small child on her hip and holding the hand of another toddler. Both children are girls and look like spitting images of the woman—especially the older child.

The woman herself is beauty, classic beauty. She's got soft golden hair that reminded me of a field of wheat growing in the Texas sun. Her skin was soft, you could tell just from looking at it and she had beauty that made you sit up and take notice. Christ, I definitely was and that hadn't happened in years.

At forty-four, I'd met enough women that beauty didn't normally phase me and I was old enough to know that more times than naught, that beauty didn't go past being skin deep. Something about this woman made me want to know if hers did.

I guess even at my age, I could still be stupid.

"You lookin' to settle down, or movin' on?"

I frown. This guy definitely is a nosy S.O.B. You gotta wonder if all people in this small town of Mason are like him. If they were, that'd be reason enough for moving on.

"Not sure just yet. Guess it depends on if I can find a job," I tell him, taking another draw on my cigarette and letting the nicotine ease the kinks out of my body.

"What type of work do you do?" he asks.

"Little of this and a whole lot of that," I respond with a shrug.

"Mommy says smoking is bad for you."

I look down to see the little girl the woman had been holding hands with looking at me. It's unfamiliar, mostly because I haven't felt like smiling in a hell of a long time, but I feel the urge to do so pull on the corners of my lips. I bend down so that I'm more at eye level with the girl, shove my Stetson up on my head a bit and give her my full attention.

"I reckon she's probably right."

"She says if you smoke your balls rot off and you die."

Shit.

I haven't laughed in a long time either, but as rusty as it sounds, I do it.

"Did she now?" I ask, still unable to contain my humor.

"Yep. That's what she told Black and Blue. Black was smoking in the hayloft. Momma told him that smoking would make his balls rot off, but if he kept sneaking up in the barn loft to do it, it wouldn't matter none."

"It wouldn't?"

"Nope, cause, he'd catch the whole place on fire and he wouldn't have to worry about rotting his balls 'cause he'd burn them off."

"Well, I reckon she probably had a point," I laugh, almost being able to picture it.

There was a time in my life that I wanted to have children, a whole house full. Turns out that wasn't in the cards for me. Maybe smoking did rot my balls, because I'm as useless as a prized gelding. It was a bitter pill to swallow, but then again, it was probably worse when my wife decided to leave after ten years of marriage. Having a child was more important to her than staying married to a man who couldn't give her that. Old bitterness, which I buried but can't seem to forget, moves around inside of me. I loved that woman, broke my back to give her a good life and in the end, it wasn't enough. Offered to adopt all the children she could ever want or need. That wasn't good enough for her. She wanted her own. Part of me understood it, but I kept trying.

Hell.

I probably would still be trying if I hadn't come in from the field early one day to find her lying on the bed, legs up in the air rutting with the owner of the bank. I can't say as it surprised me a hell of a lot, even if it did hurt. I just remember thinking that explained how I kept getting extensions on my damn mortgage.

I walked away from my spread there in Wyoming, and my wife. Ex-wife, even after all of these years that's a sour pillow to swallow.

All of that explains why, at my age, I'm drifting around Texas like a tumbleweak with no direction or purpose.

Life sucks then you die.

"AH' course to be fair, she tanned his backside so he'd know what it felt like to be on fire."

"Of course."

"Black said it worked too, cause he felt like he was on fire any time he tried to sit," the girl adds, still going. "You ever had your backside on fire?"

"It's been a while," I laugh.

"Your momma do it cause you smoked?"

"Something like that."

"Lotus Petal! You get your hind end back over here and quit talking to strangers," the woman yells.

"Okay, Momma!" she yells back.

One thing about it, God has blessed the women in that family with good lungs.

"I gots to go now," Lotus Petal calls back over her shoulder. "See ya' later, Mister."

"Later, Darlin'."

"That's Ida Sue Lucas."

"Pardon?" I ask the man.

"Ida Sue. That unruly child belongs to her. She's one in a hundred."

"She does seem like a special kid," I agree, standing back up and ignoring the pops and crackles I hear as I do it. Being a cow poke is a rough life—especially rough on the body.

"I meant she's literally one in a hundred. Ida Sue keeps poppin' them out. Course she ain't had another one since the baby was born. We're all takin' bets on when the next man will move in. Probably won't be long now. She never lets more than a couple of years go before her belly starts stretching with the next one."

"I reckon that'd be her business," I mutter, not wanting to talk about it.

"I guess so. It's shameful though. Nine kids and only two of them have the same father. I expect that's because they're twins. That one you were talking to was Petal. She's nothin' but an untrained mutt. Wild as a damn mink. All of those Lucas children are. Every last one of them."

"I see," I respond, my voice tight. I turn to walk off the steps of the small covered porch along the front of the general store.

"Hey, where you going, I thought you were coming in!"

"Decided to take my business elsewhere," I tell him, not bothering to turn around. It's either walk away or beat the asshole. I don't know the Lucas woman, but no woman deserves to be gossiped about like that. Whatever her story is, that little girl seemed happy enough. If he's an example what this town is like, maybe I should leave Mason in my rearview mirror.

4

"DOWN IN THE VALLEY, the valley so low. Hang yourself over, hear the wind blow…"

I softly sing the old song into Marigold's ear, keeping her held to my body tightly as I rock on the old rocker. I'm out on the front porch, it's warm, overly so for it to be January. I finally got my crew down—well all except Marigold and the way her eyes keep drifting shut as I sing, I figure that will be soon.

I love my kids. I love every moment with them and I don't regret having a single one of them. I also don't regret having my tubes tied once I had Marigold. I've known for a while that happily ever after wasn't in the cards for me. I figure I was cursed the day I was born, and I can't outrun the way I was raised. My parents weren't worth a damn and they didn't exactly take great care in protecting their children. I was born into a certain way of life and even if I wanted to, people wouldn't let me be anything else.

In the end, I didn't care so much. I haven't done too bad for myself, despite the hell that I've been through and I did that without anyone to lean on.

Of course, when you don't have anyone that makes it easier.

You have to learn to stand on your own and I have since sixteen I didn't have a choice.

My parents kicked me out.

It didn't matter that I was barely sixteen. It didn't matter that I had been raped. All that mattered to them was that I accused the son of one of their closest friends of the deed.

Then again, not much about me or my siblings mattered to my parents. They kicked me out, calling me a slut—a word that was ironic considering the way they lived their lives.

Slut.

That one word seemed to burn into my soul at the time. There are days it feels like it always will.

Sometimes you make choices to try and live up to words that cut you open.

At seventeen, I think I was searching for someone to love me and I ended up pregnant with White Hall.

I'd been living under a bridge at the time, with some friends. I hadn't planned on getting pregnant, it just sort of happened.

My past just left a hole inside of me. One I kept trying to fill with a different man and a new child. I believed the lies men told me, because I desperately needed to.

Lies told in the dark always have a way of finding the light, however.

Eventually, I finally realized that there are no fairytales in real life. Life is what you make of it. There is no Prince Charming riding in to save the day.

You save yourself.

Still, life hasn't been all that bad and neither have my choices. I love Texas and despite how I'm treated by most of the people here, I love Mason. The good far outweighs the bad. And although there might have been a few men in my past— although not as many as others think—there was at least one decent one.

Orville Sanders was a man among men, even with his atrocious name. He always made me smile and I loved him. Then again, I loved all the men who fathered my children—even if they didn't deserve it.

Orville came into my life after I had Magnolia—right after his brother left town because he wasn't ready to be a father. Orville was older, sweet and he might not have been much to look at, but he was damn good to me and my kids. He brought me to his farm, took care of me and my brood and didn't ask for one thing in return.

Eventually, we kissed and that kiss turned into another and another… until eventually, I moved into his bedroom. He wasn't the heart-stopping, romantic love I'd always wanted. He was steady, dependable and it was love of a different kind—one I trusted. Even then, I remember feeling scared that it would all change some day. I'd learned the hard way that men don't stay. But, Orville was different. He was also the only man to stay around when I got pregnant. When Green was born, he was as proud as a peacock, strutting around with his feathers stretched out. He didn't change, even as I braced myself and waited.

What's more, he didn't make a difference between any of my children. Green might have been his by blood, but you'd never know the others weren't as well. He loved them all.

When I had Black and Blue he insisted on adding on to his already massive farmhouse and when he did, he put my name on the deed. I didn't want that. I asked him not to, but he did it anyway. He wanted me to know that no matter what, I'd always have a home for me and our children. It was the happiest I had ever been in my life.

I loved Mason because it had become home. I finally felt like I was building a life that would make my children happy. Everything wasn't perfect. I still heard the whispers in town. They thought—and still do—that I used Orville to get his home. They all gossiped on how I slept with other men and had their babies, even while living with poor Orville. How he was too nice and he kept me anyway. It didn't matter it wasn't true, that they had no proof. All I had to do was thank the guy who cleaned our gutters and pay him. Then, suddenly we were carrying on a torrid affair.

It used to bother me, but Orville would laugh it off. He said it didn't matter, as long as we knew the truth. I held on to that —*but inside it still mattered.*

Orville was the father of six of my children and an uncle to one. I wished he had been the father to all of them. I wanted to put his name on the birth certificates, but Orville didn't want the children to have names different than their siblings. He didn't want the others to feel like they didn't belong to him too. We were in the process of hunting down Gray's father and having him sign over rights when Orville had a heart attack out in the field working with the horses.

It nearly destroyed me when he died. Some days I think it still might. Orville was twenty-five years older than me and I don't shy away from the fact that in a lot of ways he was a father figure. So, in losing him, I found myself lost and alone again. If it wasn't for my children needing me and this farm, I'm not sure what I would have done.

Orville was my rock and I'll forever miss him.

Tonight, I'm missing him a little more. It's nights like tonight when the loneliness creeps in. Running this ranch is hard work, and most days I don't get to look up from my brood to run it properly. I've put some flyers up in town looking for a ranch foreman, but so far, I'm not getting any one applying.

I heard the running joke in town was that they're afraid to apply in case they knock me up.

I may have to start looking out of town for a foreman. I hate to, because that will take a lot of time and effort, but I may not have a choice. White and Gray are older now, but they've made it plain that ranching is not how they want to live their lives. They already have begun working on careers that will take them far away from Mason. Of all of my children, the only one showing interest in the land at all is Blue. Then again, he's more like his father than any of my children. He's quiet, and he thinks of things from every angle before he acts. Orville was just like that. I swear the man could think something to death before he would act.

A fact that used to drive me crazy.

I frown at the sound of a car turning into the long driveway. It's too late for company and I never get that much anyway. I stand up and go to the door, yelling for Maggie who is camped out on the couch.

"Magnolia, get your sister and put her in bed for me. We have company," I tell her.

Maggie doesn't give me lip—which normally she would. Maybe she can hear the concern in my voice. When you're a woman alone with a house full of kids you can't be too careful. Once she takes the baby, I grab my old shotgun by the door and then make my way back out onto the porch, just as a man gets out of an old blue and white Ford truck.

I watch as he walks toward the porch and when he gets to the bottom of the steps, I motion with my gun.

"That's far enough," I warn him.

"Ma'am," he says tipping his hat. I have the porchlight turned off because of bugs, but even with just the pale light of the moon, I can tell he's a good-looking guy. Probably close to my age, salt and pepper hair and a mustache to match. He's got Wrangler jeans on with a matching jacket and a flannel plaid shirt on under it. He has a gold belt buckle that screams rodeo rider even in the darkness. If I still cared about men, I'd have to say this was one gorgeous specimen.

But I don't.

I've written men off.

From now on, it's just me and my kids.

That's it.

```
┌─────────────────────────────────┐
│                                 │
│               3                 │
│                                 │
│            Jansen               │
│                                 │
└─────────────────────────────────┘
```

"WHAT ARE YOU DOING HERE?" she asks, and as welcomes go I'd say this wasn't one, but for whatever reason I like it.

"Heard in town you might be in the market for a foreman."

Her gaze moves over me and I get the feeling she is sizing me up. I'd say it was a pretty safe bet that this woman has the instincts of a hawk. I stand here, letting her appraise me and wait, wondering just what she will see. Sometimes, I'm not so sure of what I see in myself.

"You have any experience?"

"My fair share. I used to run a spread about the size of this one for about fifteen years," I tell her. I don't bother adding that the spread was mine and that I was raised on it. There's no point.

"You have references?"

"No Ma'am."

"Can you stop with the Ma'am? You're probably older than me, so if you call me Ma'am that makes me feel like I'm older than dirt."

"Where I'm from, it's a sign of respect."

"If you've been in town, I figure you know how much of that I get."

I don't respond to that. Anything I could say won't make her feel a damn bit better.

She frowns, looking at me.

"What's your name?"

"Jansen Reed."

"What kind of name is that?"

"The kind my parents gave me."

"It's not a great name."

"Only one I've ever had. It makes me kind of partial to it."

"You look more like a tree."

"A tree?" For the second time today, I find myself wanting to grin. That should probably warn me…

But I ignore the small voice that tries.

"Yeah, something tall and lanky. Maybe Maple, possibly Hickory."

"Not Pine?"

"I hope not. The damn things leak sap constantly and ruin anything they touch. Plus, I'm allergic to it. I break out in hives with one touch. Only thing it's good for is a wood chipper."

"Suddenly, I find myself hoping you never call me Pine."

"Suddenly, I feel like I should. You staying in town?"

"Not sure. Haven't seen a hotel yet. If your job is filled, I'll probably just move on down the line."

"You're awful old to not have roots."

"I'm not much on roots."

"I guess tree might not be the kind of name for you."

"I guess so."

"You can sleep in the barn," she mutters, finally putting her gun down.

"There a room in the barn?"

"There's a hayloft."

"I can sleep in my truck," I mumble.

"Your choice. The boys head to school at seven. I can ask Magnolia to watch the girls and I'll meet you at the barn. If you manage to not screw things up, the job is yours."

"Just like that?"

"You haven't seen what I'll have you do tomorrow," she warns me.

"I guess I'll see you in the morning."

"I guess so," she says staring at me.

"Is there somewhere you'd rather me park my truck for the night?"

"Is there somewhere else you'd park a truck instead of a driveway?"

"Wasn't sure you'd like people seeing a strange truck in your driveway."

"There's something you should know, Jansen."

"What's that?"

"People are going to talk about me, whether your truck is there or not. That's just fact."

"I—"

"Hell, they're probably saying I'm spreading my legs for the horses I own."

I probably wasn't meant to, but I laugh.

"Not sure I could compete with a horse, Ma'am."

"Not sure many could. Call me Ida Sue."

"Okay, Ida."

"Ida Sue," she corrects.

"Ida Sue," I agree, but as weird as this conversation is, that name clearly doesn't seem to fit her either. "You don't look like an Ida Sue, though."

"It's a good name."

"You look more like a flower."

I don't know why, but I immediately think that was the wrong thing to say to her. She takes two steps back from me, but it feels like she's put a wall between us at the same time. It's the strangest thing I've ever experienced, but I feel it just the same.

"I'll see you in the morning Jansen. Watch out for the coyotes running around and if you get the urge to come to the

12

house, don't. I'm more of a shoot first and ask questions later kind of girl."

"So noted, Ida Sue."

"Good," she says and then she turns around, walks inside and closes the door.

I stand there frowning at the door. I hear the tumbler turn as she locks the deadbolt and then I make my way back to the truck.

Tomorrow will be interesting if nothing else. I probably shouldn't look forward to it.

But I am.

4

Ida Sue

"YOU LOOK MORE LIKE A FLOWER."

His words haunt me all damn night.

I don't know why. I figure he thinks he's being funny. I'm sure the people in town have filled him in on how I named my children—specifically naming the boys after colors and the girls after flowers. It doesn't bother me, they can say whatever they want.

There was a time I was known by *Peace Lily Lucas*. It fit, considering my parents were hippies, growing up with the generation that was responsible for psychedelic colors, Volkswagen vans, and terms like groovy. When free love was the way of the world and fighting the man was a way of life.

You would have thought parents like that would accept their daughter, no matter what. I think if I hadn't have accused someone of rape, maybe they would have. If I'd just said I had sex, there wouldn't have been a problem. Hell, they would have been proud of me. The mere mention of rape made it look like they did something wrong.

Which they did.

While they attended their parties and had their fun, my siblings and I were right there... unwatched and vulnerable.

I shrug off the old memories.

Water under the bridge.

Thinking about the past doesn't change the future. Besides if anything came from it, I know it was the resolve to make sure my children never feel unwanted or unloved. I will always do everything in my power to protect them and keep them safe… and happy. I want them happy. I want every last one of them to find their happy.

And damn if they won't.

Fairytales might not have existed for me, but they will for my children. I'll make sure of it.

Once I get Magnolia settled with the girls, I walk down towards the barn. She's off school this week and I'm glad. I know she'd rather be out with her friends than watching her sisters, but she hasn't complained. None of my kids complain very much—except maybe Cyan. My baby boy is going to be a handful for sure. He already is and he's just eleven.

"Howdy."

Jansen calls out the greeting and I immediately look around to find him. He's leaning against the side of the barn. I ignore the tingle that moves through me when I see him. I thought he was good looking last night in the dark, but seeing him now, it's clear that I had no idea. He's sex on a stick. He reminds me of old pictures I used to see hanging in the county store growing up.

The Marlboro Man.

I wanted to marry that man someday.

Fairytales.

"Looks like you survived the coyotes."

"I'm too mean for them to fool with."

"Right. I'm sure that's it. Are you ready to look over the ranch?"

"Don't you have any workers at all?"

"I used to. I had a foreman and two others. When my foreman left, he took the others with him."

"You been running this place by yourself?"

"You don't think a woman can run a ranch?"

"I'm not saying that, but you have kids."

"We can saddle up some horses and I'll show you the spread," I mumble, ignoring his response.

"You're the boss."

I'm probably a bitch, but I give Jansen Duke to saddle up. He's an ornery old cuss that doesn't like to have anyone ride him. I figure that will tell if Jansen truly belongs on top of a horse.

"What's his name?" he asks, as Duke paws at the ground, shaking his head and chomping the bit.

"Duke."

"Like a dog?"

"Like in John Wayne," I correct him, getting on my own horse.

I watch as Duke dances a few times, trying to sidestep so that Jansen can't climb on him. Jansen ignores it and seemingly climbs up into the saddle with ease.

I find myself being disappointed. I would have liked to have seen him thrown to the ground. We don't talk as I lead us out toward the north pasture and show him the small herd of cattle that I keep. He doesn't say anything one way or the other on what he thinks. I realize I need more cattle than I have, but when you don't have the men to work the land, it is what it is. Next, I take us out toward the creek bank. I used to have cattle here, but this is where the fencing is in bad shape.

"Damn. Ida Sue, this ranch needs a lot more than just a foreman."

"Yeah," I tell him and I hate that my voice sounds a little defeated.

"This fence looks like it has been years since anyone has seen to it. The barbwire is shit, and half the wooden fences are rotted…"

"I have eyes Jansen. If you think you're not up for the job, just say so."

"I didn't say that."

"Sounded like it from where I'm sitting."

"Then you need to clean out your ears. If I take the job, I'm going to need to hire some men too. Is your pocketbook going to allow that?"

"I'm not sure," I tell him, being honest.

"Can you afford me?"

"I need to get some cows to the sale and new stock in here, Jansen. The way I look at it, I don't truly have a choice."

"I think I need to look at your books, Ida Sue."

"I don't know you. Why would I let you do that?"

"Because you need me, and looking at those is the only way I'll agree to take on this job."

"That's where you're wrong. I don't need a man. I never really have."

"I'm not talking about in your bed or having my ring on your finger," he scoffs, pissing me off.

"That's good because *that* will never happen."

"I'll try not to be heartbroken about it. You going to show me the books or am I hitting the road?" he asks.

"Fine," I grumble, refusing to be hurt when it comes to this conversation. It's not like I care how he feels about me. I just need someone to help me save my ranch.

That's it.

"Fine," he says, leaning back in the saddle.

"We'll head back to the house. See if you can keep up," I taunt him and then I spur my horse into a gallop and head back home. I can hear Jansen behind me, but I don't let up and I definitely don't look back.

Duke doesn't throw him off and that just pisses me off too.

I don't know what it is about Jansen that rubs me the wrong way, but right now I find myself wishing someone else would apply for the job.

5

Jansen

I RUB the back of my neck, trying to knead out the frustration and stress. I push my chair back and look at the desk—and more specifically, the ledger in front of me. This damn place is a mess. When I agreed to take the job, I had no idea what I was getting into. I've been here for two weeks and there hasn't been a day since I got here that I haven't thought about leaving.

There's only one thing that stops me.

Correction.

Seven things.

Ida Sue has seven kids living at home, and nine altogether.

Seven.

I couldn't even imagine. If I leave she's going to lose this ranch. I know it. There's no saving it and it will be close even if I stay. The problem is, knowing that, there's no way I can just walk away.

"Mom said you might be hungry."

I look up to see Maggie standing at the door, holding a large plate with fried chicken, potato salad, green beans and biscuits. Ida Sue might be a guarded woman who can be a pure bitch. She might have enough kids to start her own football team and she is shit at running a ranch. However, there is one thing the woman can do—well, besides having kids. She can cook food that melts in your damn mouth. If I wasn't running myself ragged on the ranch trying to mend enough fences so I can attempt to buy some cattle, I'm sure I would have gained a good ten pounds.

"That smells awful good Maggie-May."

"It is. Mom is really good at cooking. It's important for a woman to know how to cook. Don't you think?" she asks, barely stopping to take a breath as she talks. The entire time, she's putting the food down on the desk and goes to the mini-fridge in the corner of my office to grab a soda, before bringing it back to me.

"I reckon it's useful for anyone to know how to cook," I laugh.

"Yeah, but more useful for a mother or a wife, right?"

"I suppose so," I mumble not really paying attention. My eyes close as I bite into the fried chicken. I thought that you couldn't get much better than Ida Sue's pork chop casserole. I was obviously wrong.

"Does your wife know how to cook?" Maggie asks, and I nearly choke as I hear the question.

I cough and wheeze and drink down half a can of soda pop before I can finally respond.

"I'm not married, Maggie."

"Do you have kids?" I frown wondering what the twenty questions is about, but I don't really care. I'm more interested in the food.

"Nope."

"Don't you like kids?" Maggie asks, sounding as if I said no the world might end.

"They're alright I guess. Just wasn't in the cards for me. Don't you have homework or something to do?"

"Yeah. *Actually*, this is part of my homework."

"It is?"

"Yeah, I'm supposed to interview someone and ask what he would look for in a wife."

"They sure have strange homework these days. Whatever happened to reading and math?"

"They still have those. This is for social studies."

"Social studies? I thought that was about maps and people all over the world kind of thing."

"Well, they want to know about people and why they decide things they do. Like who to marry. You know?"

"I guess."

"So, could you answer?"

"Answer what?" I mumble, having trouble following this conversation and wishing she'd go back home so I could eat in peace.

"What you'd look for in a wife. I have to ask somebody and the only other guy around here that I could ask would be Green and he's fifteen. If I ask him I *know* what'd he say."

"You do?"

"Yeah. He would just say as long as her legs swing open as fast as he can swing a bat."

I've seen Green swing a bat. That boy is destined for the majors so that's saying something. All I can do is laugh.

"Will you help me, Jansen?"

"Don't think I can, pretty girl. I don't know what I'd look for in a wife. I was married once and I thought she was exactly what I wanted, but it turned out she wasn't even close."

"She wasn't?"

"Nope."

"How come?"

I sigh.

"When a man picks a mate..."

"A mate?"

"A wife. When a man picks a wife, he wants someone who has a little grit about her. One who will stick with you when things go bad."

"Wouldn't he rather have someone who would make it so things didn't go bad?" she asks, innocently.

"Yeah, well, Maggie, the thing about life is that something always goes bad eventually."

"Like when Orville died."

"Orville?"

"Yeah. This was his farm. He loved Mom. All of us really. I miss him. He had a heart attack."

"I'm sorry, Maggie."

"Me too. I guess I better get back inside."

"I'll see you tomorrow, Maggie."

"Bye, Jansen."

"Bye, honey."

I watch as she walks away and I can't help but think about the man who took Ida Sue and her kids in. It's obvious he was a good man if Maggie is anything to go by.

It's a damn shame he couldn't stay and watch them grow.

I sigh.

Or stick around and save this damn ranch, because right now I need a miracle to do it.

```
┌─────────────────────────────┐
│                             │
│              6              │
│                             │
│           Maggie            │
│                             │
└─────────────────────────────┘
```

"MAGS CAN we hurry this up? I got a date," Black whines.

"You're fourteen, dick-weed. What kind of date could you have?" Green asks.

"He's got one with your Mama!" Cyan cries and we all kind of roll our eyes at him.

"That doesn't work, Cyan because his mom is ours too. Maybe you should give up the 'Your Mama' jokes," I mumble with a sigh.

"Whatever," he says, elbowing Blue.

Blue elbows him back, only harder so he falls against Green. On cue they all start rough housing and Petal starts crying.

"Will you guys stop it!" I growl, handing Petal her doll that she dropped. "We need to figure this out and do it quickly before Mom catches us."

"She won't come out here. She hates this old treehouse," Black says.

"She hates heights," Green adds.

"She sure does. Remember how she screamed like a little girl when we talked her into getting on that rollercoaster?" Blue laughs.

"She is a girl," I respond with yet another sigh. "Can we talk about Jansen and get this settled so I can get Petal inside and ready for bed."

"You shouldn't have brought Petal out here. She's kind of a blabbermouth."

"Am not, Cyan!"

"Are too."

"Am not! Mags tell him I'm not a blabbermouth!"

"You're not. Cyan will you act like you're eleven and not Petal's age?"

"This ain't going to work anyway. Mom doesn't even like Jansen. Besides I'm not so sure it's good having him around. We don't need him. I can take care of the ranch," Blue insists.

"It is a good idea. Jansen's nice and he's always doing things for us," I argue.

"Like what?" Blue argues.

"Well, last week he spent time pitching me the ball so I could work on my hitting," Green speaks up.

"And he helped me find my dolly when I lost her," Petal says.

"He helped me with my Algebra," Black says.

"He didn't help me with jack shit," Cyan says. "But I kind of like him."

"I like him too," Petal answers. "Even if his balls are rotted off!"

"His balls are rotted off?" Green yells.

"We can't be gettin' our mom no man that don't have balls," Cyan says.

"Wait. How do *you* know his balls are rotted off?" Blue asks Petal.

"Yeah. Has he been showing Petal his balls? Cause if that's what he did we'll have to kill him," Black growls.

"Yeah kill him dead," Green answers, sounding just as menacing.

"Petal, did Jansen show you his balls were rotted?" Cyan asks her.

I hold my head down, trying to figure out how to get control of my brothers and sister.

"Yep!" she says proudly, and I jerk my head up shocked.

"Oh, I'm going to kill that mother—"

"Green! Don't say that word in front of Petal," Black demands.

"Mother… *trucker*. I'm going to kill that mother-trucker," he growls.

"I'll be helping you," Blue says, his voice even darker and menacing.

"Petal, maybe you should explain exactly how you know about Jansen's… balls?" I respond, trying to get control of the situation.

"That's easy. He was standing at the store watching Mom and he was smoking."

"And?" I prompt.

"And that's it. Remember? Momma told Black and Blue that smoking made your balls rot. And Jansen is always smoking."

"Christ," Green mutters, rubbing his jaw. I try not to laugh because it hurts Petal's feelings if I laugh at her.

"I'm never smoking. I don't want to lose my balls," Petal mumbles.

"You don't have balls, Dork," Cyan tells her.

"Yeah I do! Mommy bought me a pretty purple one at the store last week."

"It's not that kind of ball," Cyan argues.

"What kind is it?"

"Let's go back to the reason we're here. We need to make Jansen and Mom notice each other."

"I still don't see why," Blue argues.

"Because Mom is sad," Green answers.

"She don't seem sad to me."

"She cries almost every night," Green says, looking at me. I frown, but nod my head in agreement.

"She really does," I tell them. They all look at me. White

and Gray might be the oldest, but they're rarely here since going away to college. I'm the one they all look to, even Green. They know that whatever I tell them is the truth.

"You think this Jansen will make her happy?"

"I do."

"Then, what do we do?" Blue mumbles, tapping his finger absently on his leg.

"We help them along," I tell him with a grin and when I look at my siblings I can tell they're all finally in agreement.

"What's our first move?" Green asks.

"We need to force them to spend time together."

"How do we do that?" This question comes from Black.

"I do have an idea… but we're going to have to be sneaky."

"Tell us more," Cyan says with a sly grin.

My brothers and sisters can be pains in the ass, but in times like this, I wouldn't take anything for them.

7

Ida Sue

"DID YOU NEED SOMETHING?"

I ask the question, not bothering to hide the fact that I'm annoyed, as I walk into Jansen's office. There's an office in the barn and attached to that are barracks that the last foreman and cowboys used. I set him up in there when he agreed to take the job on. I haven't really been here to see how he's settled in, but it looks like he's made himself at home—at least in the office.

He turns around to look at me and I really wish he hadn't. He's wearing a blue chambray shirt and faded jeans with his black Stetson. He looks good.

Really good.

If I wasn't done with men in general, he'd make my knees weak.

But, I'm done.

I'm so far done, they don't make words to describe how done I am.

"I don't think so. Nice of you to ask, though," he answers. I frown.

"Cyan said you sent him to come fetch me."

"I—"

"And while we're on that topic, do you mind not sending my

children for errands? They're my kids. If you need me then you can call the house or walk up there. You don't need to be involving my children."

"I—"

"I noticed you were playing catch with Green the other day."

"I—"

"I'd prefer if you didn't do that."

"Ida—"

"I'm sure you meant well, but that's just not a good idea. I don't want my children to begin to rely on you."

"I just—"

"I realize you didn't mean any harm. I just think it would just be better if you kept everything formal with them. They don't need to get attached to someone who is just passing through. I'm sure you understand."

I wait for him to respond. I purse my lips and keep waiting. Jansen says nothing. Instead he frowns, crossing his arms at his chest.

"Well?" I prompt him.

Still he is silent.

"Aren't you going to say anything?" I ask. I can't believe him! He could at least have the decency to reply.

"Are you saying I'm *allowed* to talk now?" he says and you can tell from his voice that he's pissed.

"Of course, you're allowed to talk."

"I wasn't sure since you weren't giving me a chance to get a word in edgewise."

"I was just making sure I was making my stance clear."

I keep my voice firm, if not a little bitchy. I'm not about to let him intimidate me.

"Oh, you're perfectly clear, lady."

"My name is Ida Sue," I remind him.

"I can see names seem to worry you a hell of a lot."

"You wouldn't understand," I mumble, ignoring the pain that causes.

"Probably not, but there's one thing you need to understand. I didn't send Cyan or anyone up to get you. I wouldn't do that. If I needed to talk to you I'd come to you, I wouldn't have you walk out here alone when there could be predators roaming about."

"Predators?"

"Coyotes? Bobcats? Hell, even a cow can be dangerous if it's escaped from the fence and trying to get back to its calf."

"I've been on this ranch for a while now, Mr. Reed, and I've somehow managed to take care of myself just fine."

"Well, I guess we've both made things clear then."

"I guess we have," I answer, but I'm wondering what we discussed at all.

"Fine, then," he says turning back around, dismissing me.

"Fine, then," I mumble.

I expect him to respond, but he doesn't. He continues working on his ledger. I stand around like an idiot for a minute or two and then, because I don't know what else to do I leave.

I don't know who Jansen Reed thinks he is, but I'm pretty sure he's the reason God gave me a middle finger…

8

Cyan

"I DON'T THINK Maggie wants us to do this," Petal whines.

"She will when she sees how good it will work," I tell Petal.

"But she said we needed to do somethin' special!"

"That's girl talk. I'm a guy and Jansen's a guy. He'll like this better, I promise," I mumble. We're standing in a supply closet at the school, watching the door to Mrs. McCallister's room.

"But what if we mess it up?" Petal whines, pulling on my shirt.

"I'm telling you this will fix everything. You like Jansen, right?"

"Well, yeah. He had a tea party with me yesterday! He even made sure Dolly drank tea too. He's nice."

"Then, we need to do this. Maggie is waiting too long."

"But she said it would be special because of Valentine's Day," she reminds me.

"That's over a week away. The way Mom keeps bitching about him, she could have him run off before then. Do you want to chance that?"

"No. Dolly would be sad. She likes Jansen."

"Then, we need to do this." I relax when I see Mrs. McCallister leave her room. She's so pretty. Whenever I pick out a woman she's going to look just like her, with pretty blonde hair and blue eyes. I even want her to wear glasses just like her too.

"But I'm hungry. It's lunchtime," Petal whines.

"We can go eat as soon as this is done," I mumble, watching Mrs. McCallister lock her door.

I was born too late. If I was just a few years older I'd be at the middle school with Black and Blue. They'd be a lot more help. I'm stuck here and the only ally I have is Petal. I could have asked one of my buddies, but I don't want them blabbing all over the school that I'm helping to get my mom a man. Everyone talks enough shit about her. It pisses me off. She's the best mom around. She sure beats the hell out of my friend Joey's Mom. She barely knows Joey's around. Everyone thinks she's great cause she never misses one of Joey's football games or his practices. Of course, she wouldn't, because she's screwing around on Joey's Dad with the coach. Yet she loves to talk about my Mom. Maybe once I get Jansen and Mom together, I can be nice and help Joey's Dad figure out what a ho-bag he's married to.

"Okay, Petal, the coast is clear. Do you know what you have to do?"

"Gee, I'm not dumb, Cyan. I stand in front of the door and if Mrs. Mc-caster comes back or any other teacher, 'specially the principal, I cry and distract them and get them away so you can hide or get away."

"Right," I tell her, pulling her hand and walking quickly to the room.

"How are you going to get in there? She wocked it."

"Locked," I correct her. Petal talks really plain, especially for someone in kindergarten. She has trouble with some words, though—locked being one of them. She's really bad with sword. It always makes me laugh because it sounds like she says turd. Reverend Slone gets really mad when she does that because he always calls his Bible his sword. The congregation laughed for twenty minutes when Petal asked him why he thought the Bible was his turd.

It was awesome.

"That's what I said," she mumbles reminding me of what I'm doing.

"Black showed me how to break in."

"He did? I wanna know!"

"Later. You watch and make sure no one comes down the hall while I do this."

"Okay, fine. But you better show me later," she warns. "You better hurry."

"I am hurrying, hush before someone hears you."

"But I need to pee!"

I ignore her and use the fake credit card I stole out of Mom's mail and slide it back and forth in the crack of the classroom door, trying to push the lock open. Black makes this look a lot easier. He's a master at it. Finally, there is a clicking noise and I can turn the knob.

"Hurry, Cyan!"

"Petal stop bouncing! I'll be right back," I growl. Little sisters are a pain in the ass.

"But, I got to peeeeee!"

"I'll hurry," I mutter. I sneak in the door, leaving the light out and walk up the aisle to Mrs. McCallister's desk. This isn't the first time I've broke in here, although Joey usually helps me. Only because he wants some of what I take.

Condoms.

Mrs. McCallister keeps a ton of them in the bottom drawer of her desk. She teaches Sex-Ed, though the school puts some big title on it like personal relationship health and education or some crap—mostly because a bunch of the parents got all pissy because we were putting rubbers on bananas. I'm just glad because I get free rubbers. I've even used two of them, which I think is really good. I mean, I'm eleven. My brother Blue is fourteen and he's still a virgin. I think Black is too, but he'd never admit it. Joey is too, which means he never uses the condoms I give him, but he still likes to get new ones.

"Cyan!" I hear Petal hiss. She really doesn't know how to be quiet. Next time, I'll just ask Joey and if he tells anyone I'll clobber him.

I reach down and grab several handfuls. I fill both my jacket pockets and my back and front pants pockets. Jansen is older though, so he might need more, so I zip my jacket and before I zip it all the way up, I throw a bunch in there. I'm just about to leave when I see the 3D diagram of a girl's thing and beside it is the book that Mrs. McCallister always brings to class. I've always liked it, because it's kind of a mystery down there and the book has really big pictures. I bet Jansen would like it too and if he doesn't I can always keep it. I grab the book and hide it in my jacket too. It barely fits, but it will work until I can get back to my locker.

I walk quickly outside, turn the lock and shut the door.

"Okay I'm ready," I tell Petal, not bothering to turn around and look at her. "Let's go." I take a few steps before I realize she's not there with me. "Petal," I whisper, although more loudly than I should and kind of urgent at that. She's going to get us caught. "Let's go!" I say again.

"I can't, Cyan," she says and she has tears falling down her face, her blonde hair all rumpled.

"What's wrong?"

"I peed," she cries. The words are somehow magical too, because when she says them she sobs and cries uncontrollably. I look down where she's standing and there's a big puddle under her. She pissed more than old Duke does.

Crap. Things are never easy with little sisters.

Never.

```
┌─────────────────────────────────┐
│                                 │
│               9                 │
│                                 │
│             Petal               │
│                                 │
└─────────────────────────────────┘
```

"IS IT READY? I saw Jansen riding out on Duke," I tell Cyan as I climb up the treehouse. I'm not supposed to climb it alone. Mom always gets mad at me. I tell her I'm a big girl now, but she just shakes her head at me. She's old, so I reckon it's hard for her to see me as grown up like I am. Adults are weird. I jump off the ladder and turn around to look at my brother. He's writing on a big box. "I thought I lost my pink marker! You stole it!"

"I didn't steal it, dummy. I only *borrowed* it. I'm going to give it back when I get this done."

"You could have ax-ed for it!" I huff.

"No point, I'm going to give it back as soon as I'm done," he mutters.

"I bet not! I bet you were going to keep it!"

"Don't be stupid. I'm a guy. What would I do with a *pink* marker."

"You can draw flowers with them and put hearts above your I's when you write."

"Guys don't put hearts on stuff, Pet."

"That's sad. I like to, but I can't with my name. My friend Sierra does, she has I's in her name though. It makes me feel bad cause I can't. Do you think Mom would let me change my name, Cyan?"

"Why would you want to change your name? Your name is pretty."

"Kids make fun of it at school."

"You want me to beat them up?"

"Nah. They wouldn't stop. Still, I wish I had a pretty name. Maybe Mom would change my name to a color like you guys. I could be Pink! Pink is a beautiful name."

"You can't be pink. I like Petal."

"You're a boy, you wouldn't understand. And I can't make hearts above an I with Petal. You know what would be really good? If my name was like Maggie's."

"I guess," he mutters not bothering to look up at me.

"Do you think she'd change names with me, Cyan? I could be Magnol-ya. That's got I's in it don't it?"

"There. The box is done," he says.

"What's it say?"

"Surprise."

"We should put a heart above the I in it."

"No, we shouldn't."

"But, Mom is the one that's supposed to be writing it right? She's a girl. We put hearts."

"Fine. Whatever," he growls, letting out a loud breath that makes him sound like a horse snorting. Brothers are always so difficult. "There! Better now?"

"Perfect! Now what?"

"Now I have to make a note."

"Are you going to write a poem?"

"No. That's just weird."

"Girls like poems."

"Well this is for Jansen and he's a guy and we don't like poems."

"Guys are boring."

"There. I finished it."

"What's it say?" I mumble, hating that I can't read a lot of words yet. I know my colors…well, most of them. I can read small words if I sound them out too. Someday I'm going to know all the words!

"It just says that Mom likes him and wants to go out."

"That's good. You're smart, Cyan."

"I know. You'll be smart someday too, Pet. You just have to get older like me."

"Yeah. You better put Mom's name on it."

"Oh yeah, I forgot," he mumbles, bending down to write on the paper.

"No! Stop!" I yell.

"What?"

"Mom's name don't start with an M. Oh! Cyan! Mom's name has an I! We can put hearts!"

"Crap. I started to sign it mom," he says, looking at the paper. Then he marks the M out and writes Ida Sue beside it.

"You didn't make a heart on it…"

"I'm not going to either," he says folding it and putting it in an envelope. He turns away from me and starts putting a bunch of foil covered squares in the box. He has a lot of them, like hundreds.

"What are those?"

"They're rubbers."

"Rubbers? Is that what they make bouncy balls out of?"

"Something like that," he mutters.

"Oh! I love balls. Can I have some?"

"No. These kinds are only for boys."

"That's not very nice," I grumble. "Boys always get the neat stuff. What do they do with rubbers?"

"It's a secret. I'll tell you when you're older," he says. I frown, because Cyan always tells me that stuff, but he never does. I'll ask Black later. He'll tell me, he always tells me stuff. While I catch Cyan putting the rubbers in the box I grab the pen he dropped and I draw a flower on the envelope. I want

Jansen to really like it, so I make it my prettiest flower ever and then I put a heart in the middle of it. I color in the petals too, cause Cyan might not think so but pink is too pretty of a color not to make flowers.

"Petal! What did you do?"

"I made it pretty. Mom would too if it was her. Don't you remember how she puts flowers on our lunch bags?"

"I guess. I'm not sure Jansen will like flowers though."

"Well, Mom does, and if she's going to like him, then he has to like her flowers!"

"Okay fine. We'll use the flowers. I don't have another envelope anyways."

"Yay! Are we done now?"

"I'm going to put a book in there I got too. I think Jansen will really like it and it might help him with Mom."

"What is it?"

"It's just a book," he says and he looks kind of weird.

"What kind of book. I like books. Our teacher reads to us every day. Mom does too."

"It's not a book you read. It mostly has pictures."

"What kind of pictures?"

"Why are you always asking so many questions? It's just pictures okay? Geez."

I start crying. It's not that I really want to, but he did hurt my feelings. Besides, when I cry my brothers usually give in and do whatever I want and it makes them feel really bad.

"What are you crying about?"

"You think I'm too dumb to see the book."

"I didn't say you were dumb, Petal."

"Then why…" I stop to sniffle, because that makes him feel worse and because I know it will, I make it extra loud. "Why won't you show it to me?"

"Fine. I don't know why you're making such a fuss. It just shows pictures of a woman."

"What kind of woman?"

"Any woman. It shows their… thingy."

"Their thingy?"

"Where you pee."

"Ew… you mean my butterfly?"

"Yeah, I guess."

"Why would Jansen want to see pictures of butterflies?"

"Cause he's a guy and we don't… we don't have butterflies."

"What do you have?"

"Uh…"

"Don't you know, Cyan?"

"Of course I know. We have worms."

"Worms? Gross. Worms are gross. Can I see?"

"No!" he growls and he must be really, *really* mad cause he turns bright red.

"Why not?"

"Cause, you can't," he says turning around to pick up the box.

"You're awful grouchy. Cyan, I don't think this book is right. This picture doesn't look anything like my butterfly."

"That's cause it's a diagram."

"What's a die-a-gram?"

"It's kind of a sketch, but not a real picture."

"Oh… it's not very good," I complain as he snaps the book out of my hand and puts it in the box.

"Trust me, Jansen will like it. All guys would."

"Guys are weird." I sigh, then I follow him down the ladder. "I'm glad I'm a girl," I add, not that Cyan is listening. I doubt he is. He rarely listens. None of my brothers do really. "I wish my name was Pink though…"

10

Jansen

LORD, I was a fool to take this job. It's the first week of February and I'm still trying to figure out how to save this damn place. I know that doesn't seem like a lot of time, but when a ranch this size is in this bad of shape it can be an eternity. I need to talk to that contrary woman about extending her mortgage, and I already know without trying how that will go over. However, that's the only way I'm going to get the spare money to replace her livestock.

Or a miracle.

Shit. Who am I kidding? It will take both.

I pour some coffee in my mug, hoping it will warm me up. I've already been out this morning riding the fence lines. The repairs seem to be holding, but I'd feel better if I had the money to replace most of those damn posts.

I'm getting too damn old for this shit. I should hang it up and maybe find my own spread again, something small. The appeal to do that is about next to nothing. Building something for the future doesn't mean shit if there's no one to do it with… or to leave it for. This sure as hell wasn't how I planned on my life being at this age.

What can you do?

Life's a bitch. Heard it my whole life and the older I get the more I believe it.

When I get my mug full, I make my way to my office. I frown because the door is open. I could have sworn I had that closed and locked when I left this morning.

I walk to my desk, my eyes more on the morning paper than on where I'm going. I all but flop down in my chair, reaching out blindly to put my cup on my desk. As it connects, something feels off, it's unsteady. I look to see what's there, because I always keep my desk clean. That's when I see a large, square box. It's brown but on the side facing me, in pink marker is one word.

"Surprise."

Weird. There's an envelope propped against it that has a scraggly flower drawn on it, in the same color pink. I open it up, still frowning.

Jansen,

I like you. Thought this would come in handy if we go out on a date.

There's a jumbled mess like she made a mistake and then her name. *Ida Sue.*

It might be the strangest note I've ever received from a woman. I'm not exactly sure how I feel about it. I mean, I'd be lying if I said I wasn't attracted to her. She's a beautiful woman, although she can be a bitch. Still, she's a good mom and it's obvious she adores her children. She works nonstop. She works cleaning other people's houses and I know she's been sewing and baking since I've been here. I haven't asked, but from looking at the books, I'm sure that's how she's surviving. There are nights I don't see the light go out in her room until after four in the morning and she has to have the kids up at six the following morning for school. I admire the hell out of her for that, especially knowing how the people in town treat her.

Still, if I had to bet, I would have said she hated me, especially after the speech about staying away from her kids. A speech I haven't really paid attention to. I don't go out of my way to talk with her kids, but the woman better think again if she thinks I'll ignore them if they come to me and ask for something. I pull the box down into my lap, opening it up—half afraid of what I'll find in there.

At first, I figure I have to be seeing things wrong. I reach inside and grab a handful and pull them out to be sure.

Condoms. Honestly, there's probably eighty condoms in this damn box.

Maybe more.

What in the ever-loving hell and tarnation is this?

Then, I notice the size on the condom.

Extra small.

Does she think she's joking with me? That I'll find this shit funny?

That's when I pull out a book that's in there. A huge hardcover book that's glossy black with white lettering on the front. The title makes my whole body freeze for a second, mostly in disbelief.

A Guide To The Female Reproduction System

Jesus H. Christ.

The woman is as crazy as a Bessie bug.

If she thinks I'm going to be the next candidate to give her a new kid, she's in for a rude awakening. I slam the book down on the floor and shove out of my seat. I don't know who in the hell this woman thinks she is, but I'm not about to put up with it. I'll give her a piece of my mind and then she can take this job and shove it. It's no wonder her last foreman ran out of town. She probably asked him to give her another kid too!

Women. There's not a one worth a damn. I don't know why I keep forgetting that.

11

Ida Sue

I CLOSE my eyes trying to focus. I've been mending this shirt for so long that I'm seeing two of my needle. Something has to give soon. I don't like who I am these days. My poor kids are going to forget they have a mom who loves them. I'm putting too much on them. Maggie is practically raising the lot of them—especially Petal and Mary. I put my sewing down and decide to go outside for a bit. The cool air may help me. As I make it outside Petal and Cyan come running in the house.

"Hey, you varmints. Where have you been this early on a Saturday?"

"I…We… Mommy, I got to pee!" Petal whines, taking off running. That child pees so much it's a wonder she doesn't float away.

"We wanted to help Jansen feed the horses, but he was already gone," Cyan mumbles. "I'm going to go back to bed, Mom. It's too early."

"But you—"

"It's Saturday, Mom," he interrupts, like that explains it all and maybe it does. I shake my head and walk outside on the porch.

I should be counting my blessings. I have a little time to myself. The other kids are all sleeping and I just put Mary back down about thirty minutes ago. She's recovering from an earache and hasn't been sleeping much at night. It will probably take me months to get that child back on a regular schedule.

I lean against the old porch bannister and watch the sun rise up in the sky. There's a definite chill in the air, but somehow just seeing the sun makes me feel warmer. I don't know what it is about a sun rising in the sky and bathing the world in its light, but it always makes me feel…*hopeful.*

"You're damn crazy," Jansen growls, jerking me out of my thoughts.

"You'll have to come up with something better than that to get my attention," I snap back, wondering what in the hell has got him upset now.

"Lady, that's just it. I *don't* want your attention."

For some reason his words hurt.

Which is crazy.

I don't want a man and I sure don't want *this* man. He's unstable as they come and I honestly have no idea what has set him off this time.

"Then why are you up here sounding like a bee flew up your ass and is stinging you where the sun don't shine?"

"I got your little *present,*" he growls and waits like he thinks I should understand exactly what that means. Then, I remember I had Green take him a piece of red velvet cake last night with his dinner. I don't usually send him dessert, and thought it would be a nice surprise.

Apparently, I was wrong.

"You're welcome?" I half question, because why someone would get bent out of shape because you sent them a piece of cake is beyond me.

"I'm forty-four," he barks.

"Okay…"

"I've been single a lot of those years, Ida Sue."

"Must be your sunny disposition," I mutter sarcastically.

"I'm not in the market to be your next baby daddy!"

I'm glad at that point that the porch post is behind me. I'm used to people whispering and spewing their venom. I ignore them and hold my head high—much like Orville taught me. Still, this time, hearing it from Jansen is painful. I didn't expect it.

"I don't remember asking you," I respond and I'm kind of proud of myself, because I managed to keep the pain out of my voice. Actually, I kept any emotion out of my voice.

"So, what was your little present about, then?" he says, his tone accusing me of something that I just can't wrap my mind around.

"I was being nice! Clearly, that was a waste of effort!" I yell, tired of this crap.

What is it with me that turns men into raving lunatics?

Raving, lying, lunatics.

"Nice? You're nuttier than a fruitcake if you think that was being nice."

"Some people would think it was very nice!"

"Then, that explains why you have a hundred kids."

I slap him. I didn't plan on it. I didn't even think about it. It was pure, gut instinct. But, I don't regret it.

Not one damn bit.

"My life, the way I choose to live it, and especially my kids are none of your damn business, Jansen Reed." I tell him, my voice so cold and quiet that I wouldn't be surprised if it began snowing around us.

I'm shaking with anger and the only solace I can find is the redness that is on his face from my hit. I curl my hand into a fist to resist the urge to hit him again. I watch as he brings his hand up to his jawline and holds it there. His eyes appraising me.

"You're right," he says, surprising me. "I shouldn't have said that."

"You damn sure shouldn't have. Maybe we don't see eye to eye on what constitutes being nice for someone."

"Well, I think that's pretty clear. I think most people would feel exactly the way I do. Have you ever thought about getting therapy, Lady?"

"Have you ever thought about what it would feel like to have buckshot in your hind end? Because you're about to find out."

"You beat all I've ever seen," he mutters, yanking his hat off and running his hand through his hair. I refuse to think that's sexy in any way, shape, or form.

"Listen, I need you to work here on the ranch, at least until I can find a replacement. I'm pretty sure you need the job or you wouldn't be here."

He doesn't reply, but I push on through.

"Let's just make a deal for now. I'll make sure I don't go out of my way to be nice to you and you stay away from me. We'll only talk about the ranch—that's when we have to talk at all, and that's it. Can we agree on that?"

"Fine. As long as you get it through your head that I don't want to be the next in line to give you a kid."

"I'm not planning on having more kids! Jesus, I can't anyway!"

"Then, what was the gift about?!?!" he yells back.

"How does a piece of cake make you think I want you to knock me up?" I ask, exasperated.

"Cake? What are you talking about?"

"I sent you a piece of red velvet cake last night. Didn't you get it?"

"Cake? Well, yeah, but that's not what I'm talking about… *Unless…* Was that part of warming me up, too?"

"Warming you up? You really are insane. I wouldn't warm you up if it was Thanksgiving Dinner and you were the turkey!"

"That makes no sense at all."

"I don't have to make sense!"

"Well that's damn clear!"

"Do you think you could tell me what has you so upset?" I sigh, that headache I had earlier starting to throb.

"That damn box of condoms you left on my desk!"

"Condoms?" I ask, thoroughly confused.

"Exactly that! Along with that damn book on the female... *you know*!"

"I don't think I do know."

"That damn book you left to explain where the female watch-a-ma-jigger is!"

I hold my head down. I'm smelling rats here and it is rats about the age of eleven and five.

"Let me get this straight. You somehow got it in your head that I sent you a present of condoms and a book detailing the female... *area*—"

"There's no point in denying it, just because I'm confronting you about it. You signed it for damn sake. If you're going to send something like that at least own up to it."

"I don't know who signed *it*, or whatever, Mr. Reed, but I can assure you, it wasn't me."

"What? Then why—"

"I have no idea, but I intend to find out. Still, just for the sake of argument here, let's say I did send it. How would me sending you condoms make you think I was trying to make you become a daddy? Seems to me the opposite would be true," I tell him logically.

I watch as his face changes slowly, and embarrassment creeps up it. Then he narrows his eyes, beats down that emotion and annoyance flares back up on him.

I don't know how I can read him that clearly, but I can.

"As long as we're clear that I'm not a candidate to be your—"

"Trust me, I wouldn't think of you as a candidate to do anything for me except run this ranch," I respond, my voice is once again cold.

"Fine then!"

"Fine." I cross my arms at my waist and wait for him to leave—or say something else to piss me off.

He looks at me, his frown increases, and then he slaps his hat back on top of his head and turns to leave. He stomps off about three steps before he stops. When he turns back around to look at me, his eyes are narrowed.

"I'll have you know I am not a size small."

I blink, so sudden is the topic change that I don't understand.

"I don't—"

"You women are all the same. You think a man only has one role in your lives and that's not fucking true. I might not have fathered children, Lady, but I know how to use what I got."

"Mr. Reed—"

"And it might be worthless when it comes to making babies, but it sure as fuck ain't small! It's big! You got that?"

"I—"

"*Really* big!"

He turns around and leaves after delivering that.

There's a lot to take in from that. I'm not sure I understand it completely, but I get the idea that Jansen might have had the same luck with women that I used to have with men. I'm even pretty sure he has his own scars to deal with.

Scars that need fixed.

But, that's not my job.

Not in the slightest.

Jansen Reed is not my cow.

Not my cow, not my pasture, and not my meadow muffins. Therefore, not my concern.

Petal and Cyan though? They are and they've got some explaining to do. I turn to go back inside.

It's going to be a long ass day.

"Petal? Cyan? You two get your butts down these stairs right now!" I yell, forgetting I have a sleeping Mary to worry about.

When she starts crying through the monitor I want to cry myself.

Yep.

A long freaking day.

Maggie

"I THOUGHT I told you two not to do anything until we told you!" I hiss at Cyan and Petal.

"We were only trying to help," Cyan mumbles.

"Yeah, we were only trying to help. We like Jansen! We want him to be our poppa!"

"Well, he's not going to be your poppa. We already had a dad," Blue says, and I can hear the anger in his voice, and I can understand it. He's been the one most resistant to fixing mom up with Jansen, and probably because he remembers our dad the most. All of us do, but Dad and Blue were a lot alike. They were super close. I don't mean he didn't love us all the same, he did. But he and Blue just had some kind of connection. Blue loves the farm and ranching life as much as Dad did, they bonded over it. Blue even joined the F.F.A. and Dad never missed a chance to brag on him.

"We did have a dad, a great one," I tell him. "But, Jansen would be good to have around, too, Blue. He'd make Mom happy."

"You don't understand," he mutters and he stomps off, walking back toward the house.

The rest of us are gathered on the creek bank. I frown as I watch Blue go.

"He'll be okay. He's just missing Dad."

"I miss him too," I tell Black.

"Yeah, but he wasn't your Dad. Not really," Cyan says.

"He was, in all of the ways that counted and he loved us all," I respond, repeating words Mom preached to us when we were in school and the kids would make fun of us. I smile at him and he smiles back—even if it's kind of a sad smile. "We'll always miss Dad. That doesn't mean we can't love Jansen too. Especially if he makes Mom happy and she stops crying all the time," I remind them.

"And working so much. I miss her," Petal whispers.

"I do too," Green mutters. We all kind of mumble our agreement. At least we can all agree on that.

"Then, we need to work together—not go off and do things without getting everyone's approval."

"Fine," Cyan grumbles.

"I don't think it's going to work now," Black says. "It's been three days and they haven't even spoken to each other. Mom has even stopped sending Jansen down supper."

"Yeah," I sigh. "Maybe we should just give up."

"Nah. They just need to talk things out. Whenever my girl-friend gets pissy, I always set her down and we talk it out."

"Your girlfriend is a bitch," I mutter before I can stop myself. I swear all of my brothers have horrible taste in women. They think with their dicks, that's the only reason I can come up with at all. White is the worst one of all of them. He's a total horn dog. My friend Kayla thinks he's everything, but she's too young. White doesn't even look twice at her.

"She is, but she has some good things about her," Green says with a wink.

"Gross," I mutter. With brothers like mine, it's no wonder I'm still a virgin at seventeen.

"I'm just saying, arguments can almost always be worked out if you just get them to talk things out alone," Green says.

"You're not talking about talking. You're talking about fu—"

"Black!" I yell, to stop him from saying fuck, because Petal is close by and can hear him. Black jerks his head around to look at me and I motion toward Petal.

"You're talking about…." He doesn't finish, clearly unable to come up with another word for fucking.

"About hiding the sausage," Cyan says, helpfully.

I need to kill my brothers. They know entirely too much about sex, too!

"Why would Mommy and Jansen want to hide sausage? That's gross. I did that once in my room. I was in trouble and I wanted to go outside. Mom said I had to clean my plate, but I wasn't hungry. Remember Mags?" Petal says.

"I remember. Let's—"

"I hid my breakfast under my bed, but I forgot," Petal sing-songs, proving that all of my siblings, male and female, are wanting to kill me off.

"And it stunk really bad. Mom got mad cause there was bugs and stuff."

Everyone snickers, while I just hold my head down.

"Mom and Jansen don't need to hide the sausage, eggs, bacon or anything else they might have for breakfast," I mutter, narrowing my eyes at my brothers. "They just need to talk. Anything else would be gross."

"And cause worms. That's what happened under my bed!" Petal adds.

My brothers lose it and snicker, like the juvenile delinquents they are. I might laugh too, if I wasn't so worried about how to get Jansen and Mom to makeup. I really believe that Mom would be happy again with Jansen. I really need for her to be happy before I go away to college.

"How are we supposed to get Mom and Jansen to talk?" Black finally asks.

"I got an idea," Green says and from the look on his face...
I should probably be scared.

The sad truth is, however, I'm running out of ideas and after
the mess Cyan made of things, I'm more than a little desperate.

"Fine. What do we do?" I ask Green, knowing I'm going to
regret asking.

"I got it all planned out," he brags, grinning widely.

Yep... I'm so going to regret this....

"JANSEN? What do you think makes a good woman?" Green asks out of the blue.

"Haven't thought much about it, I guess, son."

"Mags says my girl is a bitch," he says flopping down on the chair in front of my desk. His long, lanky legs stretch out and he perches his foot on the corner. I give up all pretense of working and look at him. There's one thing I've learned about these Lucas boys—and girls too, really—once they have something on their mind, you might as well let them speak their piece.

"Maggie seems like a pretty good judge of character," I hedge.

"Yeah."

"So, is she?"

"Huh?"

"Is your girl a..."

"Bitch? Yeah," he laughs. "She totally is."

"So, you're wondering if that says she's not a good woman?" I ask. I swear being around these kids is making me feel younger. Although, I can't remember my brain going in as many directions as these kids for sure.

"Maybe, I guess. So, what do you think makes a good woman?"

"I reckon, that's different for every man. I'd wager to guess what I think is important and what you do are pretty different."

"Why do you say that?"

"I'm older than you. I'm not out there looking to…"

"Get laid?" Green answers with a smirk and I lean back in my seat, taking the boy in.

"I guess that's so. My Dad taught me to be a bit more respectful than that though."

"Hey, I respect women. I love women."

"Love in my time, boy, meant a lot more than getting my rocks off."

"I—"

"I'm not getting after you. You're young. Too damn young to understand that sex is a whole lot more than the act—or at least it should be."

"Jansen—"

"Women are special, no matter who they are. The way you think about this girl of yours. Is that how you'd want someone to be with your sister, or your mother?"

"But, it's *not* my sister or mother."

"It's somebody's." I tell him and wait for that to sink in.

"I like my girl though. She's pretty. She's the captain of the cheerleading squad."

"That's good. If you're going to waste time with someone, it's good you like them."

"Is that what you're looking for Jansen? Someone you like?"

"Well, I don't really see me looking at this point in my life."

"Why's that? You're not old."

"Some days I feel older than dirt," I laugh, not even kidding. "But, I had my shot at love once. It didn't work out. Too old now to be twisting myself up over a woman. That's a young man's game."

"Maybe you can find a woman who don't twist you up," he

says and that makes me smile. He doesn't know it yet. He's young. I don't have the heart to break it to him that all women twist you and bend you. He'll find that out on his own.

"Maybe," I laugh. "Your game still on for Friday night?"

"You know it," Green grins. The boy has an arm on him like I haven't seen. He's going to go places, and he has no idea how far. He's got big things on his horizon. "You going to come watch me?"

"I'll be there. Got to see if you put that extra twist in your curve ball."

"I'll do it. Just like you taught me," he says sounding excited and his words cut inside of me deeply. I never had a son and I never will, but if I did... I would have wanted to teach him how to throw a curve ball. I would have loved to go to his games, too.

"Can't wait," I tell him, clearing my throat because suddenly I have way too much emotion inside of me. Green gets up to leave and he's almost out the door when he stops to look back at me.

"I'll make you proud, Jansen. Wait and see," he says and damn it... Those words mean more than I could ever tell the boy.

14

Ida Sue

I'M SO STUPID.

For the hundredth time, I'm calling myself a fool and trying to talk myself out of doing this. Jansen will probably just say something to piss me off. I shouldn't even bother trying—especially after our last conversation. I stare at the strawberry cake I just made and want to groan.

I'm sooooo stupid.

I made this for Jansen after hearing Maggie and Petal talk about how much Jansen loved the strawberries they picked him from my garden. I swore I wouldn't do anything nice for him again—not after the way he acted about Cyan and Petal's little surprise. How a grown man could think I'd send him a box full of condoms and pictures of the female's reproductive system is beyond me. It'd almost be funny except for one thing...

The knowledge that two of my youngest children are trying to set me up with a man.

I had to talk plain with them, and I only hope they listen. At the very least, I'm hoping they're afraid to matchmake anymore because as it is, they won't be allowed to leave the house except to go to school, for at least a week.

I went down to Jansen's office to explain what had happened

and that's when I heard him and Green talking. His words struck me so deep I couldn't breathe. I never had a father who cared enough to give me heart to heart talks. Orville did and until I heard Green talk with Jansen, I had forgotten how special that bond could be. Jansen didn't have to do that, but he took the time to gently teach my son. Green's smart. I know when the time is right the seeds that Jansen sewed will take root. So... I wanted to thank him.

By baking him a cake. After our fight and the talk about me sending him dessert.

Admittedly, the fight between us really had nothing to do with the piece of cake I sent him. But still...

I'm so, so, so, sooo stupid.

I'm also nervous, which is crazy. The trip to Jansen's quarters doesn't take long, but it feels like forever. I try to talk myself out of it a hundred more times, but out of pure stubbornness I keep going, holding the strawberry cake like it's a dang shield.

When I get there, Jansen's door is open, so I knock on the door trim instead.

"Have you got a minute?"

Jansen turns to look at me. He's wearing a white shirt under a blue jean jacket and faded Wranglers today. He doesn't have his hat on and his dark hair is rumpled, streaks of gray around his sideburns and along the edges. I wish I could quit noticing how good looking he is. It'd be better all the way around if I could. He takes off his reading glasses and nods at me.

"Sure."

"I... Well, Maggie and Petal mentioned you liked strawberries. I had some left in my greenhouse... I thought..."

"Ida Sue—"

"I wanted to apologize. Well, I mean not for me, really. More for my kids. It's just—"

"Cyan told me."

"He did?"

"Yeah. He came down the next day and explained he put the box on my desk and wrote your name."

"I didn't know."

"Yeah, I figured that out. I went off half-cocked. I don't do that much anymore, but I did this time. Children… well the having of them… it's a sensitive topic for me, I guess. You kind of got caught in the crossfire of that. I'm…" he clears his throat. "I'm sorry."

"I am, too. I don't know what got in their heads."

"I suspect they were trying to get us together."

"Yeah. Before you ask, Mr. Reed, I didn't tell them to, or give them any—"

"I never thought you did. I'm learning kids pretty much have a mind of their own," he laughs.

"Ain't that the truth," I murmur, joining in with his laughter as I put the cake on the desk.

"That's a mighty-fine looking cake," he says, making me grin.

"I could cut you a piece?" I offer.

"Ida Sue… at the risk of upsetting you again…"

"Are you about to accuse me of something else?" I joke.

"I'm allergic to strawberries," he says looking really uncomfortable.

"What? But… The girls…"

"Well they picked me a handful of those things and I couldn't hardly say no, especially when little Petal was so proud of them."

"You ate them?" I gasp.

"Well, yeah."

"You ate strawberries, knowing you were allergic to them?" I ask again, not quite believing him. "What if you had died?"

"I took some allergy medicine and it's not like a major allergy. I mostly break out in hives and itch like a… mother… like a pig that's been rolling in poison oak," he finally says, clearing his throat and blushing. I can see the color on his face.

"But, that's crazy. What are you going to do if they bring you more strawberries?"

"I'm hoping considering the time of the year and all, you might not have anymore?"

I grit my teeth because I have quite a few more in my greenhouse. Jansen reads my face quickly.

"I guess, I better stock up on allergy meds," he says with a weary sigh.

"I...I'll get rid of them."

"Nah. I wouldn't ask you to do that. You work hard in that greenhouse. In fact, you work hard from sun up to sun down. You need to learn to relax a little."

"What's that old saying? I'll rest when I'm—"

"Dead," he adds, with a small laugh. "Still, you need to enjoy time with your kids. I know you've been working extra because of money, but you need to take some time to enjoy life instead of making yourself old before your time."

"There are days, Mr. Reed, that I feel ancient."

"Mr. Reed was my dad. Call me Jansen."

"Jansen," I murmur and like I'm some damn school girl—not a woman almost forty—I can feel heat rise on my face.

"I like that," he says and I start to ask him what, but I don't. Maybe, I'm afraid of his answer.

"Are you really going to Green's ballgame this weekend?"

"I was planning on it. Is that okay? I know you asked me not to get around your kids, but—"

"I say a lot of things when I'm mad, and most of them are foolish. It would mean a lot if you go to Green's game. To him, I mean. It would mean a lot to him."

I stumble on the words, feeling like a silly school girl.

"Then, if you're sure, I'll definitely be there."

"Sounds good. I guess I'll head back to the house... Uh... with my cake."

"I'm sorry, Ida Sue..."

"Don't be. The kids will eat it after dinner tonight, it will be gone before you blink. I still feel bad…. Uh… Would you… I mean, you don't have to… but, you're more than welcome to come up to the house and have dinner with us."

"I'm not sure that's a good idea. Your kids might think I've set my cap for you."

"We'll make it clear you haven't," I tell him.

"It might encourage their matchmaking…" he warns.

"I'm brave if you are."

"I'll see you at dinner," he says. I'm almost out the door when a thought occurs to me.

"Mr. Ree—"

"Jansen," he corrects.

"Jansen, uh… are you allergic to apples?"

"I love apples," he says, looking at me strangely.

"Good to know," I respond. I turn to leave, and I have the strangest urge to skip all the way to the house.

I resist.

Barely.

15

Jansen

I COULD ALMOST ALLOW myself to pretend that this was my life. It's certainly the life I always imagined. A house full of loud children. A woman—a good woman—cooking dinner and laughing, clearly showing she loves her kids. It would be good to pretend.

Just for a night.

This is not for me, though. It was never in the cards. I need to remember these kids aren't mine. This home is not mine and that woman… that woman is definitely not mine. The problem is, the more I try to remind myself of that fact, the more I want to ignore it.

"Mr. Reed? Do you want more pie?"

I look up as Ida Sue asks me that question. My stomach is about to bust, I ate so damn much. The fact that she made an apple pie after already having a cake though, makes me smile at her. She made that damn pie for me and I have to admit that it's the best tasting one I ever had.

"I couldn't hold another bite, but I might take one with me, if it's not too much trouble."

She smiles, doesn't reply, but a man could get used to the warmth in her eyes. I rub the side of my jaw, letting my fingers scratch through the scruff. I don't want to leave, but I know I need to. Ida Sue is one hell of a woman. Would it be so bad to claim her as mine? Take care of her and her kids? She needs someone. This ranch might not be mine, these kids aren't mine, but they need someone.

Why couldn't I be that person?

Ida Sue may deserve better than a broken-down, old cow poke, but I could bust my ass and make this ranch operable again. With some luck, prayers and hard work it could make money. It's a daunting challenge, sure. But, if Ida Sue was the reward, her and these crazy kids, it'd be more than worth it.

"Mom, do you know what you haven't done in a while?" Maggie asks.

"What's that?"

"Sit outside and enjoy your coffee. You should tonight. You and Jansen. Green and I will clean up the kitchen."

"We will? I don't do dish—Ow!" Green stops talking and ends with a yell when his sister kicks him under the table. I hold my head down, so they can't see me silently laughing. "Yeah, okay, fine. We'll clean the dishes for you, Mom. You go sit outside and drink coffee," Green mutters, glaring at his sister.

"I'm sure Mr. Reed has other things to do," Ida Sue responds giving her children a scowling look.

"Actually, I'd like a little fresh air," I tell her, standing up and reaching out my hand to her. She looks down at it and me and I'm pretty sure I can see panic on her face. I expect her to turn me down, but she surprises me. Her hand goes in mine.

We walk outside and the door barely shuts before we hear the kids cheering loudly.

"Score!" Cyan yells. "I think he likes her!"

"Of course, he likes her, dummy. Our mom's a babe!" Black says.

That does make me laugh and I don't even try to hold it back.

"I'm going to kill them," she mutters, holding her head down.

"Well, they are right about one thing, Ida Sue."

"What's that?" she asks, still looking down at her feet.

I cup my hand on the side of her neck, applying enough pressure so she'll look at me.

"You are a babe," I murmur, looking into eyes that are a shimmering green that I'm pretty sure I could lose myself in.

16

Ida Sue

YOU WOULD THINK a widow of thirty-eight, with nine children, would know how to be comfortable in her own skin. You would think she could handle herself around a man. The sad truth is, I lost myself the day Orville died and I just haven't been able to find myself again. If I'm truly honest with myself, I lost myself before that.

Orville just held me together.

"I'm really sorry about this. I'll have a word with them after you leave," I tell him, kind of wishing the ground would swallow me whole.

"I'm not sorry. I had a real good evening with you all. It was fun."

"I think you're mistaking fun with loud," I laugh, taking a step back from Jansen. I'm getting drugged by his scent, by his presence.

"Maybe it was a little of both," he says with a shrug, his hand falling away.

"I'm still going to strangle them."

"You got good kids, Ida Sue. Really good kids."

"They are. I haven't done a lot right in my life, but my kids are my world. I'm proud of them."

"Why would you say that?" he asks.

"What do you mean?"

"What do you mean you haven't done a lot right? From where I'm standing, you've done a hell of a lot."

"Jansen, I'm barely keeping a roof over my babies' heads. You can't have missed that since you've been knee deep in the books for the last month. And I'm sure you noticed the portable plastic patio table we are using to have supper on, or the big pot in the corner that we keep there because the roof is leaking."

"Doesn't change the fact you have good kids and you've done a hell of a job raising them, Ida Sue."

"I guess," I mutter, suddenly uncomfortable.

"I *know*," he says. "Look at me, Ida Sue," he orders quietly.

"You're an amazing woman," he says. He leans in towards me and I'm caught in his stare. He's going to kiss me. My heart speeds up and it wouldn't surprise me if it didn't pound out of my chest. I feel my body swaying, moving into him and my eyes begin to close.

"Dude! He's going to kiss Mom!" Cyan yells. I look over Jansen's shoulder to see all seven kids with their noses pressed into the picture window.

I drop my head against Jansen's shoulder, which is shaking with his laughter. I feel his hands rest on my sides and they feel like they're branding me.

"Can I kill them?"

"You'd regret it."

"Maybe," I sigh. "I should probably go back inside. Being out here with you is not discouraging them…"

"I like having you in my arms," he whispers softly against my ear.

"You say that now, but how will you feel if Cyan and Petal bring you more presents?"

"I can deal."

"We really should be careful about encouraging whatever

they have cooked up in their minds. Trust me, I know my kids, they can be scary, Jansen."

"There it is," he murmurs.

"What?" I ask, pulling away just enough to look at him. He has the deepest brown eyes. A girl could totally lose herself in them.

"You finally said my name. I've been Mr. Reed all night. I like Jansen coming from your lips much better."

"The kids are watching," I remind him, rolling my lips together, wetting them because my mouth is suddenly dry.

"I want more time with you, Ida Sue."

"I… I have nine kids, Jansen."

"So?"

"I'm kind of a mess."

"A beautiful one. No prize myself, Lovey. The way I see it, you don't get to be our age and not have some kind of mess in your past."

Lovey.

It's a strange nickname, but I like the way it rolls from his tongue. I like the way it sounds and I'd be lying if I didn't say that the tender way he says it makes my knees feel like jelly.

"But the kids…"

"We'll have to be creative and keep it from them."

"Creative? Have you met my children?" I laugh, startled with his answer.

"You haven't seen me in action yet, Sweetheart. I'll give those whipper-snappers a run for their money."

"I don't think I can spend time with a man who calls my kids whipper-snappers," I warn him.

"I'll make you like it," he winks, pulling away. "I'll see you tomorrow, Ida Sue."

"Tomorrow, Jansen," I tell him and he walks backwards to the edge of the porch, his gaze locked with mine.

"Yeah. I really like my name on your lips, Ida Sue. I truly

do," he says, then he turns around and walks down the steps. I watch him walk away and as he disappears into the darkness I barely resist the urge to squeal like a damn teenager.

"HEY, MAGGIE." I call as she walks through the door and deeper into the barn.

"Hi, Jansen. Kayla and I were wanting to go riding. She's spending the night with me tonight."

"Howdy, Miss Kayla."

"Hey, Jansen," Kayla says shyly. She's a pretty little thing, a bit timid, but a good kid. Kayla's been here at the farm often. Ida Sue has pretty much claimed her as one of her own. She's hopelessly star struck on White and always talking about him when she's here. She's way too young for him, and I hope she gets over her crush before she gets much older. If not, then she's bound to get her heart broken.

Young hearts.

They're full of energy, but more than a little stupid. Then again, I may just be an old fool.

"Your Momma know your plans?" I ask Maggie.

"Um… Well, no. But, we always go riding, Jansen. I can ride a horse better than I can walk," Maggie answers.

"Just the same, run up to the house and let her know what you got planned and where you are going."

She frowns at me. "We never did before, Jansen," she says stubbornly.

"But, he's right. You should," Ida Sue says coming through the doors.

She looks pretty as a picture today. Wearing jeans and a simple white T-shirt, but she looks better than a woman dressed to the nines. My ex used to spend hundreds of dollars on a dress to go out to dinner. At the time, I thought she was beautiful. She couldn't hold Ida Sue a light to go by right now—no matter what she was wearing. Ida Sue has her hair pulled back in a pony tail and it's hard to decide if I should watch the way it bounces with each step she makes or the gentle swell of her breasts and how they sway as she walks. I decide on her hair—just because there are little ones around us.

"You're never here, Mom," Maggie says and I see this look come over Ida Sue's face and I know the simple words hurt her. She definitely needs someone to help her before she drowns in work and bills.

She needs me.

"Thank you," Ida Sue says softly once we get the girls saddled up and on their way.

"For what?"

"Having my back. Maggie doesn't like answering to anyone. It's been that way since she graduated high school early and began taking college classes. She got an invite from the Dean of the college to stay on campus for a week to see if she'd like to go there full-time next year. They offered her a scholarship. I probably shouldn't have let her go. Ever since, she tries to act like she's an adult, which I guess she mostly is… but…"

"But, she's your baby and it's common courtesy to tell you when she goes riding so you know where she's at. She's still under your roof, Lovey."

She colors a little bit and laughs.

"What?" I ask.

"Lovey?"

I rub the scruff of my beard looking down at her, contemplating my next move here. I'm out of practice bad when it comes to courting a woman.

"You don't like it?" I ask.

"I didn't say that. It's just… unusual."

"My Dad called my Mom that. I guess it just slipped out without me realizing it. You remind me of my mother in a lot of ways."

"Was she the talk of the town, too? Did they want her to wear a scarlet letter A on her dress and be marched about?"

"If the town bothers you that much, why don't you move?" I ask her.

I put my hand at the small of her back and we start walking back toward my office which is at the end of the barn beside the tack room, from there it connects to my quarters—and the other hands, if I can ever manage to get enough money to hire the ones I need. I take her to my office. It's safer to talk there. There's a bed in the other area, and that's too much temptation. I think Ida Sue likes me, but she seems as spooked as a horse that's never been saddled. I need to take my time.

"It bothers me, but mostly for my kids. This old house is home and it's the one my kids love and have memories of. When Orville died, I remember them crying wondering where we would go and if they would like their new schools. White, my oldest, told them we'd have to leave the house. He just assumed we'd move now that Orville was gone. It was an honest assumption, and truthfully I did move every time a relationship fell apart and unfortunately there were a lot of those—not just with their fathers."

"I'm sorry."

"I have penchant for jumping in things too soon and a gift for attracting slores," she mutters.

"Slores?" I laugh, leaning against my desk and standing beside her.

"It's a combination of sluts and whores."

"I think those terms are used to refer to women," I respond with a smirk. "I'm not really sure what they call men…"

"Slores works. They whined like little girls, anyways, and definitely had PMS more than I did."

"I don't have PMS," I tell her, still grinning.

"Most people who have PMS, never admit to it or see it for themselves. Sorry Jansen, the jury is still out," she answers and there's a spark in her eyes that I've seen glimpses of before, but I see it full on now and damn if I don't like it.

"Well, I'm definitely not a… *slore*. There's been very few women in my past, Lovey."

"Even if there has been, it doesn't mean you're bad, you know. What makes you bad is if you had those women at the same time," she says, her face earnest.

"Very true."

"I never did, in case you were wondering. I was always in it for the long haul. They are the ones who just ran."

"They were idiots."

"Mostly, yeah. Although there's a part of me wondering if it's not me."

"Ida Sue—"

"Something inside of me that makes me unworthy of their attention, of their love," she says, looking off in the distance. The look on her face is thoughtful and sad and it looks like she's drifted off into the past because there's definitely pain there. I can read that clearly, because I have some of my own.

I curve my hand around the side of her neck, bringing her focus back to me.

"I don't see anything but beauty," I tell her honestly. She stares at me for a long moment, those shadows of the past still in her eyes and then, just like that, she shrugs them away.

"Anyway, when I saw how upset my kids were, I couldn't leave. This was home. I swore I'd never leave it and they'd always know that this was their home."

"It would have been easier to move somewhere else, some

place smaller with more opportunity job wise for you," I respond, still taking notes on Ida Sue and liking everything I uncover.

"Easier isn't always better, Jansen. Most of the time, easier is the road you regret taking."

"Ida Sue?"

"Yeah?"

"I'm going to kiss you now."

"Do you always tell a girl you're going to kiss them before you do?"

"Only when it really matters."

"Oh…" she gasps, right before my lips takes hers.

18

Ida Sue

IF YOU WERE to ask me how I got back to the house, I couldn't tell you if my life depended on it. I might have danced. I felt that good after Jansen's kiss. It's strange that at thirty-eight I can feel like I've been kissed for the first time in my life, but that is exactly what it feels like.

I make it in the house and then I lean against the shut door, with my heart beating crazily in my chest.

He kissed me.

It was a damn good kiss, too. It was the kind that makes your knees weak and clouds your mind. The kind that sears inside of you in a way that you know you will remember it for the rest of your life. The kind that makes you forget every kiss that came before it and will probably be the one you measure any others that come after it.

I sigh like a silly school girl, which I'm not and haven't been in a long time. I never even finished high school. I didn't get the chance. I was too busy trying to survive.

"What's going on with you?"

I look up to see my oldest son, White, eyeing me closely. I don't let myself react.

"What do you mean?" I mumble.

"You look…."

"Winded. I ran all the way back from the barn. I'm late to get over to old Mrs. Waverly's."

"I hate that you have to clean that old cow's house, Mom."

"I think you just insulted cows," I joke lamely.

"I'm going to go pro next year," he declares.

"You are not."

"Mom—"

"Don't you Mom me, White Hall Lucas."

"You said you'd quit calling me that," he says with a wince.

"It's a good name, but don't distract me. You are not leaving college early to play football."

"We need the money—*you* need the money."

"I'll survive. I always do. It's important for you to finish your schooling."

"I can always finish later, Mom."

"We both know you won't."

"Of course, I will."

"White Hall, you're lyin' like a no legged dog," I chastise. "You hate everything about school."

"That's not true. He likes the part where he gets the girls," Gray says, coming in.

"I do like that part."

"I can quit, Mom," Gray says.

"You won't either. You both are going places and I didn't work my butt off so you could give up on your dreams."

"But you're broke," Gray says. "I can—"

"I might not have a pot to piss in, but I still have a window to throw it out of. I'm not that desperate just yet. Jansen's been working here on the ranch and if the price of beef holds, we may turn in a profit next month," I tell them, not bothering to say how small. Still, being in the black is better than the red any day of the week.

"Green's been telling us about this Jansen. Who is he exactly? Can we trust him?"

"He's been working hard and he has good references. I'm not senile just yet, I know how to hire someone to work. Now, quit changing the subject. What are you two boys doing back in town?"

"Aren't you glad to see us?" White laughs.

"Always, but I wasn't expecting you."

"Green invited us down to watch his game tonight. We decided to meet up in Dallas and drive down."

"You had money to spare for that?" I ask them, knowing money is as tight for them as it is for me. They both got free rides to college for sports, but they work part time to cover everything that doesn't cover. I know it can't be easy for them, but they do it without complaint. I've made a hell of a lot of mistakes, but my kids…

They are everything.

"We're fine, Mom. You need a ride into town to that witch's house?"

"White," I chastise, laughing.

"Where you going?"

"She's cleaning Mrs. Waverly's house today," White tells Gray.

"God, I hate that old woman."

"It's not good to hate people, Gray."

"She's a bitch, though."

"Still, don't let her be a blot on your soul, son. She don't matter."

"Whatever," he says.

"It's true, it doesn't even matter that her nose is so far up in the air that she would drown in a rainstorm," I joke with a wink —making them laugh. "I could use a ride. It'd be nice to have my two handsome boys escorting me into town."

"White will have to take you, Mom. I promised the twins I'd take them to Shuckey's for Pizza."

"Oh, let me give you some money and I'll let you pick up—"

"I'm already getting it for everyone. I don't need money."

"Son—"

"Mom, it's fine, I swear. I'd tell you if I didn't have it. Now go before you're late."

I hug him, closing my eyes and letting the happiness fill me. I miss my boys. I miss them every damn day. I'm glad they're seeing to their dreams and reaching high. It makes me proud. It doesn't make being away from them any easier, however.

White links his arm in mine and I follow him out and to his old beat up truck.

"Love you, Gray," I call over my shoulder.

"Love you, too, Mom," he says and I smile, squeezing White's arm.

"I love you, too, White Hall."

"Same goes, Mom, but honestly, drop the Hall, please?"

"It was a lovely hall. Did I tell you? The ceilings had wood beams…"

"La-la-la-la, I can't hear you!" White yells and I laugh. My kids think I got their names from where they were created. I invented colorful stories to make them smile. They're little harmless white lies that give them roots. I want that. I want their laughter and their joy in memories. Plus, it's damn fun to poke them with a stick and watch them squirm.

The truth is much less… *enjoyable.*

I named my boys after colors because most of my life it felt like I was barely existing. I wanted my kids to have beauty and to be surrounded by color. I wanted them to have everything I didn't. It began with White. The hospital walls were a sanitized white. I'd look out in the hallway and see that white paint and pray my parents would walk in the door, apologize and promise to love me and take care of me. When that didn't happen, I prayed White's sperm donor would come in and offer to help support me and the child while I got on my feet.

That didn't happen either.

When the nurse asked for a name to put on his birth certificate, I remember staring at that white hall and vowing that my boy would have joy and color in his life. I named him White Hall as a reminder to myself to always strive to give him more and to not waste my time on wishing for others to do it. I would have to be enough for White.

I obviously didn't learn my lesson. By the time I had my second child that damn wall was Gray. When I had my daughter, I thought maybe I should concentrate on something besides the wall. Besides naming a girl Yellow—which was the wall color, although a different wall and state than where I had my boys—just didn't seem right. There was a giant Magnolia tree outside the window though.

Yeah. I never want my kids to learn the truth to their names.

I'd rather watch them smile and laugh and act uncomfortable when I prod them and do my best to make them uncomfortable.

If I'm honest, it's one of my favorite things to do.

19

Jansen

"SO, YOU'RE JANSEN."

"Last time I checked," I respond, rubbing the side of my neck. The guy in front of me looks to be in his twenties. He looks a little familiar, but I don't remember seeing him before. Obviously however, he knows me.

"I'm White."

I frown for a minute, thinking he's telling me the color of his skin. It's not like that would be a great mystery. Then, it hits me.

"Ida Sue's boy."

"I don't think anyone's called me a boy in a long time... 'cept maybe my coach."

"When you get my age, that changes. You're lucky I didn't call you a kid."

"I guess so. How do you like working on the ranch?" he asks, moving to stand beside me and imitating my stance by leaning toward the fence, his hands on the top of the pad that is over top the steel post that connects the chain link.

"It's a job," I answer. Wondering what this conversation is about.

"Green and the others really like you, Jansen."

"I like them. They're good kids."

"What about, Mom? You like her too?"

"She's a good woman."

"She's the best. That doesn't really answer the question," White says. I look out over the field where Green's game is about to start. Wasn't really expecting this would start my night. Then again, I kind of thought I would have seen Ida Sue before now and so far, she hasn't shown up either.

"No offense, White, but what I feel or don't feel for your mother is kind of between me and her."

"Fair enough. I'm just letting you know Mom takes a lot of shit from people in Mason. There's not a lot I can do about those close-minded idiots. But, I'm not about to let anyone else get away with it."

"I can respect that. If it makes any difference, I think your mother is a hell of a woman."

"It makes a difference—"

"White Hall Lucas. What in damnation do you think you're doing?"

I lean my head down and hide my smile while I contain my laughter when I hear Ida Sue.

"Mom, I told you about that name—"

"I'd like to know what you think you're doing talking to Jansen."

"I'm just trying to look out for you, Mom," White mutters and suddenly he sounds just like a little boy getting chastised by his mother.

"I ought to set your ears on fire. I've been taking care of myself for a damn long time."

"You're not alone anymore though, Mom. Gray and I are old enough to help now and—"

"And nothing—"

"Ida Sue, leave the boy alone."

"The hell I will. Jansen you've had my kids—"

"Ida Sue, I'm telling you to leave it alone. I love your kids and I respect White for seeking me out."

"You're about as smart as a screen door on a submarine yourself, then."

I laugh. I probably shouldn't. What man would laugh when the woman he's set his hat on insults him?

Apparently, I do.

"Lovey, you're late, you've almost missed the start of the game."

"I went over to Rick Mullins's after I got off."

"What did you go to that asshole's for?" I growl. I've been in town long enough to know that Rick is the owner of the store, and the one I met when I first came into town. It still don't sit well with me how he insulted Ida Sue and talked about her.

"I see you've met the dickhead," White laughs.

Ida Sue slaps him on the back of the head instantly.

"Shit, Maw—"

She slaps him again.

"Keep going and I'll keep hitting."

"I'm done, I'm done," White says grudgingly.

"The boy's just telling the truth. He is a dickhead. Why did you go and see him?" I demand, not bothering to hide my frustration.

"He wants someone to clean his house."

"Hell, no," I growl at the same time White does.

"I don't think I have to have permission from either of you."

"Damn, did Green and Cynthia break up?" White asks, with a long whistle, changing the subject abruptly.

"Yeah, he broke up with her a day or so ago. He's been talking to—"

"I see who he's talking to. Damn she's a babe. Little brother has good taste. What's her name?"

"Lord, White. That head injury you had the other day caused more damage than we knew," Ida Sue mutters.

"It wasn't a head injury. I just got the wind knocked out of me when I got tackled at practice," he responds, not even bothering to look at his mom. "Seriously, who is that hot little piece?"

"Her name is jail bait, son. She's just turning fifteen," I remind him.

"She's got curves that are much older. Green never dates girls younger than him, which means this girl could be seventeen. That makes her legal."

"She's dating your brother, son. *And,* she's a good girl."

"I like good girls, Jansen," he grins. "I like them even more when they can be bad, too."

"Son, that's not a good way to think about a woman, any woman really. But that girl—"

"What Jansen's trying to tell you, and you're missing—seeing as how your tongue is watering the grass and you can't pick it up off the ground—*is* that girl is way too young for you and it's also Kayla," Ida Sue interjects.

"Kayla who?" he asks, still looking at Green and Kayla talking.

"The Kayla who stays with your sisters?"

"*Our Kayla?*" White squawks.

"I think she might be Green's now. Black said Green was going to ask her out."

"*Our Kayla?*"

When Green leans down to give Kayla a kiss—admittedly a mostly chaste one, but it looks sweet—White growls under his breath.

"Green knows better than to play with Kayla. She's a kid and had too many hard knocks," he says walking away, not bothering to say goodbye.

"That going to be trouble?" I ask Ida Sue, figuring she'd know. I can't help but wonder if White and Green will get into it over Green dating Kayla.

"I hope not, Kayla will be the first girl I actually don't mind Green talking to. But honestly, who knows, life is never dull with my brood."

"That's true," I murmur, watching as White walks up to his brother and slaps him hard—a little too hard—on his back and interrupts his private time with Kayla.

"I love my boys, but I swear, sometimes it's like the porch light is on but nobody's home, especially when it comes to girls."

"Got it," I tell her, finally understanding. "They're young. Boys don't exactly think with their brain at their age," I tell her.

"You sound like you're speaking from experience," she laughs.

"Sadly, I am. I know you worry, but they're good kids. They'll figure things out eventually."

"Probably, but Kayla will probably get hurt by Green in the meantime."

"Now, that'd be a shame."

"I agree."

"What's this about you going to work for that horse's ass in town?" I ask, bringing the conversation back around.

I don't care what I have to do, there's no way Ida Sue will be working for that man.

20

Ida Sue

I LOOK AT JANSEN. His good-looking face set as if it was carved in stone. It almost makes me smile. I've seen stubborn up close before, I see it in my own face when I look in the mirror, not to mention the faces of my children. For some reason, seeing it on Jansen's face makes me feel warm inside. I'm not sure why, except that it feels like he's concerned about me and that hasn't happened in a long time. Still, it doesn't matter how Jansen feels about things. I don't have a choice. I need this job. Besides, I like Jansen and his kisses are nice, but I've learned the hard way that you can only depend on yourself in this life.

"I'm taking the job," I tell him, to head off any argument.

"That man is an ass," he grumbles.

"Maybe, but he has money and I need the job."

"The ranch made a small profit this month."

"Very small. Listen, Jansen. I appreciate your concern, but it's not your place."

"Ida Sue—"

"My kids will always come first. If I have to scrub that asshole's toilet to make sure they have food on the table and a roof over their head, then I will. I'd do it if he was Lucifer himself. So, it's done."

"He's probably worse than the devil," Jansen grumbles.

"Can't argue with you there."

"He has one time to make a move on you and I'll introduce his face to my fist."

"Did you really just say that?" I laugh.

"I did and I mean it," he says, his voice definitely showing he's not happy.

"Can we just enjoy Green's game?"

"I been thinking about that," he says, moving in closer to me.

We're not touching, but I can feel the heat of his body close by and I'd be lying if I said I didn't like it.

"About what?" I question, my voice dropping down as a wave of desire moves slowly through my body. It's been a long time for me, but Jansen is waking up feelings I haven't let see the light of day in forever.

"Why on earth are they having a baseball game in February? I thought baseball was played later in the year."

"Well, the regular season starts around the end of March or sometime in April. But, Green's team always has several early games in February. The coach says scrimmages give them time to get used to the grind."

"I thought Texas was a football state."

"We're a multi-talented state," I laugh.

"I'm starting to learn that," he says his voice soft and throaty. The look in his eyes intense.

"Jansen?" I ask, proud of myself because his name doesn't come out squeaky. Especially since his stare seems so hot and passionate it could set me on fire.

"Yeah?"

"Are you… I mean are you…"

"Am I what, Lovey?" he says his voice barely more than a murmur. His hand comes up and his thumb slides against my chin causing goosebumps to rise over my skin and shivers of awareness to slither through my body.

"Are you…" I start again, and then realize I don't know exactly what to ask. So, I decide to go a more direct route. "What are you trying to do to me?" I ask, my gaze locked with his.

"What does it feel like?"

"Like you might be trying to seduce me."

"Is it working?"

"Probably, but it's been a while for me, I'm probably not much of a challenge. I'm currently thinking about getting into a committed relationship with the rinse cycle on my washing machine." I tell him with a frank honesty that would probably be better stifled.

It obviously surprised him because I watch as his eyes widen, then those full lips of his spread into a smile on his rugged face and a bark of laughter explodes. It's such a beautiful show, I instantly wish I could replay it over and over.

"That's real damn good to know, Lovey," he says, still laughing.

I shake my head and turn to look at the ballgame. Jansen moves in closer, and I feel his arm go around me. I hold myself perfectly still for a minute and then slowly relax into him.

He surprises me by kissing the top of my head.

"You're quite a woman, Ida Sue."

I ignore the quickening of my heartbeat and the small voice inside of me that says Jansen is one hell of a man himself.

21

Jansen

"WHERE DID YOU PARK?"

I'm walking hand in hand with Ida Sue toward the parking lot. The game was a good one and Green showed that he is definitely the star of his team. I enjoyed the night, but mostly because Ida Sue stood by my side and in my arms through most of it. It's been a long time since I've held a woman that close and it was so much better than I can ever remember. Although, to be honest, I'm sure that mostly had to do with the fact that it was Ida Sue.

When we first met and even up until lately, the woman was wrapped up so tight I would have thought she was going to explode. Now, even though she's still timid, I'm starting to see other qualities, traits that she kept hidden. Traits that answer something deep inside of me. She somehow feels new and exciting while feeling familiar and welcomed altogether.

Like coming home.

Not sure I've felt like this since I lost my parents.

"I didn't," she says, bringing my attention back to the present.

"How did you get here?"

"I walked. The ballfield is literally a twenty-minute walk from the house I was cleaning."

"You walked alone?"

"Well, yeah," she laughs. "I had a good time tonight, Jansen."

"It's dangerous for a woman to walk alone, Ida Sue," I mutter, not liking the idea of her being alone and unprotected. Not liking it at all.

"I'm a grown woman, Jansen. I can take care of myself."

"I don't like it. Where's your truck?"

"Maggie wanted it for the night."

"Ida Sue—"

"Will you stop? I'm a grown woman. I'm fine. Stop being annoying and ruining our date."

"Our date?" I ask, allowing her to distract me, but only for a little bit.

"Well, you had your arms around me most of the night and we're holding hands. I'm a little rusty at the whole dating thing, but I think this qualifies."

"I'm a little rusty too, but in my day a man picked a woman up and took her out for a nice meal for it to be qualified as a date."

"Well, you did buy me a hot chocolate and a chili dog," I remind him.

"If that's what you call a good meal you're the easiest woman I've ever met."

"I've been called that before," she mumbles and I want to kick my own ass.

"Ida Sue, that's not what I meant."

"I'm just stating a fact. Don't get your knickers all bunched up."

"There's two things you need to know about me, Lovey."

"What's that?" she asks as we make it to my truck.

"First of all, it might be old fashioned, but in my world a woman doesn't walk alone anywhere. It's too dangerous and some people are evil to the core." Her face jerks up to look at me and there's something in her gaze that I can't name, but I don't think I like it.

"What's wrong, Lovey?"

"I think I just discovered that I like old fashioned," she whispers.

"That's really good," I murmur, leaning down to take her mouth.

I didn't plan on kissing her, not right now in this crowded parking lot. Not with all the people around that already love gossiping about her. I just can't seem to stop myself.

This kiss is different from our others. Every kiss with Ida Sue is good, but they've been slow and sweet. Ida Sue has been tentative and I haven't wanted to rush her. This is different because she opens for me immediately, her tongue moving inside my mouth, searching. My hand wraps in her hair, curling the long lengths around my grip and holding her as I take over. I explore her mouth, urgently. It's been a long time since I've needed to kiss someone as much as I need Ida Sue. I'm not a young kid anymore, not someone who is just kissing because it feels good. This kiss has everything to do with hunger, hunger for Ida Sue.

I feel her hand move along the side of my face, and her fingernails teasing against my scalp as she tries to pull me even deeper into our kiss. She needn't have bothered. We can't get any closer. Our tongues are dancing, ravishingly mating.

Without thought my hand drops down to her breast and I slide along the underswell, stretching my thumb up to seek and find her nipple. It's hardened, tight and pebbled against her shirt and although I know she has a bra on I moan at how good it feels, despite the fabric in my way. I press against the nub, wishing I could taste it.

I force myself to break away, my eyes still closed as I hold her close, and listen to the way our ragged breathing combines into a rhythm that sounds beautiful to me.

"I really like old fashioned," Ida Sue murmurs against my chest.

My lips stretch into a smile.

"I'm really damn glad to hear that."

"What was the other thing, Jansen?"

"What do you mean?"

"You said there were two things I needed to know about you," she reminds me.

It takes me a minute to think about our conversation and when I do, I pull away and lift her face so her gaze is on me.

"I don't wear knickers," I respond with a grin.

She gives me an exasperated look as if she's rolling her eyes at me.

"Boxers, briefs, whatever, Jansen."

"Don't wear those either."

Her eyes go wide and then drop down to the crotch of my jeans. I don't know if she can tell through the denim, but my cock is definitely hard and pressing against my zipper.

"Damn, Cowboy," she says, looking back into my eyes, making me laugh despite being so hard I could hammer nails.

I shake my head and help her into my truck.

"You're one hell of a woman, Ida Sue Lucas. One hell of a woman," I tell her, giving her a quick kiss before closing the door.

I'm starting to believe coming to Mason, Texas was the best decision I have ever made in my life.

The very best.

22

Ida Sue

"DOES THIS COUNT AS A DATE?" I ask Jansen as he spreads the blanket I brought with us. He puts it under my favorite oak tree. It's a huge oak out from the small stream. It happens to be my favorite place on the ranch. When Orville was alive, I'd pack up a huge basket of food, make it big enough for a meal with the kids, and we'd have lunch with him. It's some of my best memories.

"Technically not, since you provided the food, but I think we're definitely getting closer," he jokes with a wink, making me laugh.

"Well, whatever. I'm glad you asked me, just the same."

"You dressed up for me," he says, and damn if I can't feel myself blush. A woman at thirty-eight, shouldn't be able to blush—not if you'd lived my life.

"Not really," I halfway lie. I don't normally wear dresses. Today I'm actually wearing a soft pink t-shirt and a white skirt which flows out in layers. It falls about mid-calf. There's nothing sexy about it. Then again, I don't own sexy clothes. I never have. The urge to wear those died in me when I was raped. Still, I wanted to look nice for Jansen and I did try. It feels good that he noticed.

"You look beautiful," he says and there goes that blush again.

"I hope you're hungry. I packed enough food in here to feed an army," I tell him, trying to distract myself by pulling the basket over to open it.

"I'm starved," he responds, his voice so deep it sends chills over me.

I instantly stop what I'm doing and look up at him. He's bending down to sit on the blanket beside me, his eyes boring into me and heated. Anticipation runs through my system like a wildfire and I can feel my heartrate increase.

"Jansen…"

"Definitely not for food, Lovey," he murmurs, the same intensity in his voice, but it drops down in volume, making it more seductive. He reaches over, grabbing the basket and moving it to the side as he settles in and pulls me into his arms.

I go willingly. I'm not sure I can do anything else. I've completely fallen under Jansen's spell. I don't know how it happened. I have no idea how he slid under my defenses. There've actually been men that have tried since Orville died. Some were probably good men, I just didn't want men in my life anymore. I had my babies and that's all I needed… all I still need. It's just, Jansen reminds me that I'm a woman. He even manages to somehow remind me of the girl I once was… before life beat me.

And it did beat me.

"I've been wanting to do nothing but kiss you for two days straight. Ever since I brought you back from that baseball game," he murmurs, his lips so close that his breath feathers across my skin.

"Why didn't you, Cowboy?"

"The only time I've seen you, you've had your children with you. So, I've been biding my time, slowly going insane."

"We're alone now," I murmur.

"That we are, Lovey. That we are." His hand moves under

my hair to slide against the side of my neck as he pulls me the small distance between us. He kisses me, gently at first—which is always Jansen's way. Then, quickly, the kiss intensifies, growing heated as he takes over my mouth.

Somehow, in the midst of tangling tongues, pressing lips and teeth crashing as the kiss grows fiercer, I find myself lying with Jansen over me. His body stretched over me, heated, warm, *commanding.*

Finally, we break apart, and I do it gasping, dragging oxygen in my lungs. Jansen's breathing is just as ragged, but he buries his head in the curve of my shoulder, his beard tickling against my neck.

"Better than I remembered," he says in between small kisses on my neck.

"Definitely."

I don't know exactly when it happened, but I've managed to pull Jansen's shirt from his pants where it was tucked, and my hands are underneath it, holding him to me, my nails dancing gently back and forth on his back. I think I can feel his heart beating rapidly, but that could be mine—because it's definitely running away from me.

Jansen keeps kissing my neck before tenderly moving to my shoulder, kissing it, letting his teeth drag against the sensitive skin.

"You're a drug, Lovey, and I'm definitely becoming addicted," he murmurs into my ear. "Your skin is so soft and sweet, it tastes like honey."

"Do you like honey?" I ask, inanely.

"Never doubt it, Honey Girl. Never doubt it," he says pulling back to look at me. His eyes are crinkled, he's wearing a relaxed smile and, in that moment, I know.

Jansen will be the one man I never recover from.

Because, one day he will leave.

Everyone always leaves...

23

Jansen

I DIDN'T SEE it coming. This pull I have for Ida Sue, hit out of the blue. I thought I could control it. I thought I could explain it away, but it's clear I can't. The more time I spend with her, the more I lose myself. I wasn't lying to her when I told her I was becoming addicted. She's the first thing I think of when I rise in the morning and the last thing I think about at night. Her laughter seems to live inside of me and I can hear it at the oddest of times, despite being completely alone. Her smile lives in my head and when I close my eyes… it's there. Smiling bright.

For me.

I'm not much to look at. Don't have a pot to piss in anymore. Got some money in the bank, but mostly I live from paycheck to paycheck. I gave my ex the house, the land, my cattle and even my damn dog. I couldn't have kids, the woman I loved didn't want me because I was half a man. There was no point in holding on to anything. So, I walked away from everything and I never mourned it, not for a minute. Right now, I find myself regretting it. If I had kept the land, kept the house, I would have had a good place, a refuge for Ida Sue and her kids.

I'd have had things to offer this beautiful woman, who deserves the world.

Instead I have nothing but me. And again, I'm not much. I'm much less than she deserves, than those crazy kids of hers deserve.

"What are you thinking, Cowboy?" she asks, her voice soft and lazy.

"That you deserve better than some broken down old cow poke with nothing to offer you," I respond truthfully.

Her hand comes up to brush against my face and she lets her fingers play in my scruff. I like it. I like it anytime she touches me, but I decide right now with her eyes soft, her lips bruised from my kiss and her teeth nibbling on the corner of her full lip… I like it even more.

"Have I asked for anything?"

"Maybe you should," I tell her.

"Tell me about you."

"Me?" I asked, surprised.

"I want to know."

"Not much to know, Lovey," I tell her moving my body off of her so I don't hurt her. Then, I move, positioning us so that her head is in my lap and I'm sitting up while she's lying down. It gives me the best view in the world. She reaches up and grabs my hand and our fingers slide together, resting on her chest, near her breast…

Near her heart.

"Tell me anyway," she says smiling up at me. I think, if she keeps smiling at me, I'd tell her anything—*do* anything.

"I'm not much more than a drifter, Lovey. Been that way since my marriage broke up and that's been more years than I can count. Been searching ever since."

"What are you searching for?"

"Now that's the million-dollar question," I laugh.

"What's the answer?"

"I was raw after my marriage broke up. Took a lot of years

to break away from it, I guess. Even when I did, it left scars that I suppose will always be there."

"You still love her?"

"Nah. That horse has been dead a long time."

"Then, what scars?"

"She wanted kids. I couldn't have them. She found someone who could give her what I couldn't."

I watch as what I said registers with Ida Sue. Her soft face shows shock, and her body goes solid for a minute, tensing up. Then, she blinks and her eyes narrow.

"She left you because you couldn't... because you..."

"Shoot blanks," I answer and it's weird, but even after all these years that still hurts. I would have said once that I had no ego, but I know now that's wrong. No man wants to be thought of as less, and that's how my ex thought of me and in many ways, that's how I think of myself. I can't help but wonder if that's how Ida Sue will see me now.

"Your ex is an idiot."

"I think that sometimes, but the truth is she wanted kids."

"Then, you search for a solution or you adopt. You don't leave a good man, because it's not possible the old-fashioned way."

I stare at her a minute, feeling surprised all the way to the tips of my boots.

"What?" she asks, when I can't help but continue to stare at her.

"I'm just surprised you feel that way."

"You shouldn't be," she says shaking her head. "I'm a lot of things, Jansen, been accused of even more, but one thing I'm not or could never be called is shallow."

"But, obviously, having children was important to you," I remind her.

"I love my children, I'm not saying I don't. I'd lay down my life for any of them in a heartbeat and not ask questions. But, each time I had a child, it was because I was looking for something to heal a wound made inside of me that I figure will never get healed. Especially, since I kept looking in the wrong places."

"Tell me about the wound."

"I don't want to upset you, but… I'm not ready to go there just yet, Jansen. I'm not sure I ever will be," she says so quietly that I have to strain to hear her.

"One day you'll tell me and one day, Lovey, I'm going to find a way to heal you."

"That's a really nice dream," she says her face a little lost… and a lot sad.

"It's a promise," I correct her.

"Do you think anyone can heal you, Jansen?"

"I'm forty-four, Honey Girl, not sure it's possible to teach an old dog new tricks."

"Then—"

"But, if anyone can do it, I think it'd be you, Ida Sue."

She holds my gaze for a minute, and then lowers her eyes to look at our joined hands. She squeezes mine a little tighter and when she looks back at me there's some unnamed emotion that I really wish I could pinpoint.

"I wish I'd have met you when I was younger," she murmurs.

"Maybe it wouldn't have changed anything," I tell her, knowing in my heart that it would have.

"Maybe it would have changed everything," she says and I kiss her, not deeply, but I kiss her, because I have no words to tell her how deeply that affects me.

She seems to understand, because when we break apart there are unshed tears in her over-bright eyes. I clear my throat from the sudden onslaught of emotion I'm feeling and Ida Sue seems to recognize that too, because her grin instantly becomes sassy.

"I know one thing for damn sure."

"What's that?"

"I probably wouldn't have had as many kids."

A startled bark of laughter forces its way out as she surprises me. How she can make something that has left me raw inside seem funny, I have no damn idea. It's just part of her charm, and only one of the reasons I keep wanting more and more from her.

"Damn, Lovey," I finally respond, shaking my head.

"I'm kidding mostly. I couldn't imagine a world without my children, even if they do drive me crazy."

"They're good kids," I tell her, definitely understating how I feel about them.

"They are. They seem to have given up trying to fix us up, which is good."

"They already know I'm panting after you like an old blue tick hound, begging to have his belly scratched." She rolls her eyes, but laughs and I close my eyes and let the sound seep into me. "Besides, how do you think I found this place? Definitely not by chance."

"The kids told you about my favorite spot?" she asks, her voice thick with shock.

"Maggie to be exact. She says this used to be your favorite place for family picnics."

"Well, it was… I just didn't realize they knew that."

"Your kids are very perceptive, Ida Sue. I doubt they miss much, even little Petal."

"Probably not. Cyan is the rounder. I've spoiled him, because he was my boy. He's way too wild and untamed. I try to keep him reined in, but I'm not sure it's possible."

"He's a good kid. I'm afraid he's in for some hard truths someday, however," I agree.

"Yeah," Ida sue replies, sounding less than pleased.

"There's no sense biting off more than you can chew right now, Lovey. There will be time enough to worry about Cyan later," I tell her with a wink, wanting to steer the conversation away from anything heavy.

I lean back on the old oak tree at my back and listen to the water run in the stream across from us.

"You're right," she finally agrees, and I feel her relaxing, her grip easing on my hand.

"Why is this your favorite spot?" I ask her, hoping to keep her distracted.

"That old oak tree behind you," she says easily.

I look to the side trying to see the wide trunk and then I look up. It's a huge tree, towering over the land and sheltering it at the same time.

"You have hundreds and hundreds of trees on the ranch." I don't quite get why this one is special, even though it is impressive. Still, I want to hear from her why it is; I find I want to know everything to do with Ida Sue.

"Maybe. But this tree has stood the test of time. Look at it's roots? They're not only solid, they've grown into its own surroundings and become part of it all. Do you see how they've grown out of the earth, so big you could sit on them? It has history, and you know it's seen a lot, weathered a lot of storms, and yet it's still solid. It's special."

"Like you," I murmur, my voice thick, suddenly seeing that old tree as much more than a tree.

"Not hardly, but it's what I'd like to aspire to be, I suppose. That old tree never fails to make me feel safe and comforted when I'm here. I come down here to contemplate my circumstances," she grins.

"Contemplate your circumstances? What exactly are they, Lovey?"

"I think it's a fancy way of saying feeling sorry for myself, but it makes me feel better."

We laugh together, staring at the tree.

"It's a good tree."

"It is. It's a forever kind of tree, a mighty oak." She nods. "I wanted to carve mine and Orville's initials in it once, but he wouldn't let me."

"Why's that?" I ask, unable to stop myself.

"He thought it was silly, and maybe it was. It just felt like putting something on that old tree… might have made it…" she breaks off as if she is searching for words. "Might have made it something that old oak would deem worthy to protect. Make it something that would last. I guess, hearing myself say that, it does sound kind of silly."

"I don't think so, Ida Sue. I don't think so at all."

"You don't?"

"Nope. I think we should put our names on it."

"But we… I mean… According to you, we haven't even gone out on a date."

"Ida Sue Lucas," I chastise.

"What?"

"Are you scared?"

"Of course not," she rebukes.

"Prove it, then, woman. Put your money where your mouth is."

She frowns at me.

"I don't have a knife."

I help her up and then get up myself, all while reaching down in my pants pocket. I pull out a pocket knife. "Who's first?" I dare, as her eyes go wide. I don't know why it's important but suddenly I want our initials carved in this old tree more than anything I've ever wanted in this world.

She takes the knife from my hand and I grin at her. Slowly, her smile appears and her face relaxes.

She turns and carves her initials. *I. L.*

Then hands me the knife. She can try to wimp out, but I'm not about to let her. I get to work on my carving and it takes me a little longer.

But then I make a heart around her initials and I add a plus sign before putting my own initials under that.

"Jansen…"

"Something sustaining, Ida Sue. Something worth protecting," I remind her. I watch as the delicate muscles in her throat move as she swallows.

"Something… real," she answers, her voice barely more than a breath of wind and yet it feels like it gives me wings.

"Something real."

24

Ida Sue

"DO YOU WANT MORE POT ROAST?"

Jansen looks up at me with a smile on his face. A smile I'm beginning to love. A smile I already dream about. It's crazy to me how I've only known him a little over a month and my days already revolve around him so much. It's probably not healthy. I should try to control my feelings and rein myself in.

I'm not doing that, however, and right now I'm not sure I can.

I think it might be too late.

"Lovey," he says, leaning back, his hands on his stomach. "I think if I tried to eat another bite, I'd explode."

I grin at him and we share a smile.

"I'll have more, Mom," Blue says and I ladle a heaping serving out to my boy.

"Me too," Black says.

"You already had three plates full," Maggie mumbles.

"I'm a growin' boy. Besides I think I'm going to try out for the wrestling team this week," Black says, around a mouthful of food.

"Black, don't talk with your mouth full," I chastise automatically. I always do, and it never does a bit of good.

"Sorry, Mom," he mutters—his mouth exploding with roast, potatoes and carrots, I might add. I just shake my head. With kids, you have to know when to pick your battles.

"You wouldn't make it on the wrestling team," Blue grumbles.

"I'll show you little brother."

"Stop calling me that moron, we were born at the same time," Blue mutters.

"Blue, stop calling your brother a moron," Maggie reprimands, sounding like a mini-me.

Damn I really have been relying on her too much lately.

"You always say that, but we weren't born at the same time. We know I came out first and obviously got the good looks."

"Too bad you didn't get the brains," Green mutters and gives Blue a high-five. Jansen pretends to cough to hide a laugh.

"Whatever," Black mutters. "Blue's just scared I'll beat him," he adds and then looks over at Blue. "It's okay, you should be scared. I'm totally going to whip your ass," Black brags.

"Don't say ass," I tell him, before Maggie can. Jansen grins and shakes his head at me.

"You will not."

"Will too!"

"Fine, if you think you can, let's prove it right here."

"Fine bring it on," Black says standing up. Blue rises up slowly too, his face somber, eyeing his brother like prey and he's a wolf.

Shit.

"No. Absolutely not. Do you two not remember what happened last time you wrestled in my kitchen?"

"Aw, Mom. Come on."

"I said no. You want to be dummies, go outside, but you are not ruining another table. It might be plastic and on its last legs, but at least it works."

"Fine. Let's go outside."

"It's cold out there," Black whines.

"Either you're tough enough to wrestle or you're not," Blue reasons. I swear sometimes I think that child might be a grown man inside a child's body.

"Fine. We'll wrestle outside," Black mutters. "Who's going to judge us? Jansen?"

"Uh…"

"Nope. Jansen is helping me with the dishes," I tell them, speaking up. Jansen jerks his head over to look at me and smiles.

"Dishes? But, Mom! Jansen's a man. You can't make him do women's work!" Green complains.

"Women's work? Where do you get off calling it women's work, you moron," Maggie yells, offended for all of womankind. I should probably remind her that she just got onto Black for calling his brother a moron. But Green's asinine comment did make him sound like a moron so I let it go.

"I like doing dishes," Jansen, speaks up.

"You do?" All the kids ask this in unison, clearly not believing him.

"You give me a choice between doing dishes with a pretty girl or going outside to watch you two roll around on the ground when it's barely forty-five outside, I'll pick dishes any day of the week."

"You think Mom's pretty?" Cyan asks.

"Prettiest woman I ever saw," Jansen says, looking at me.

"I think he's been hooked," Petal whispers—*loudly*.

"Petal—"

"Well, that's what you said, Green," Petal responds. "You said Mom's the bait and we got to get Jansen on the hook and reel him in slowly."

Green looks really uncomfortable and I might take pleasure in it, if I wasn't currently able to glow in the damn dark. My kids are going to be the death of me.

"Petal—" Green tries to quieten her again, but he doesn't get very far.

"And I think he's hooked! Hey Jansen?"

102

"Yeah, pretty girl?" Jansen, says laughing.

"Are you going to be our new daddy?"

"And, that's enough. The lot of you go outside or to your rooms," I speak up, my face so hot that I could fry a damn egg on it. "Maggie you take Petal up and get her ready for bed, while I clean up."

"Okay, Mom," Maggie says, taking her sister's hand. "You really need to learn how not to be a blabbermouth," she chastises.

"I'm not a blabbermouth," Petal denies. Then she runs to Jansen and jumps into his arms. "Night, Jansen!"

"Night, little one," he says, hugging her tight. He kisses the top of her head and something about that makes my heart hurt… but in good ways.

"Who's going to decide who wins the wrestling match?" Black says demanding attention again.

"Yeah," Blue agrees. "We need a referee."

"Yeah, come on Jansen! Come ref for us!" Green says.

I shrug at Jansen, when he looks at me—letting him decide.

"I better not. I need to spend more time with your Mom. Make sure I'm on the hook *really* good," he says with an easy grin. My mouth falls open slightly. I should tell him that encouraging my kids is dangerous, but I can't find it in me to warn him.

"What are we going to do for a ref then? Maggie's with Petal," Black says, clearly upset he can't try and prove he can out wrestle Blue.

"What about Green?" Jansen asks.

"He'll cheat," Black says.

"I'm sure he won't—"

"Yeah, I probably will. Blue doesn't brag if he wins at something. Black never shuts up," Green admits.

"Cyan can be the referee," I tell them. "And if they don't listen to you, spray them down with the garden hose," I tell him.

"Heck yeah!" Cyan screams as the boys go running from the kitchen.

"You yahoos be quiet before you wake up Mary," I warn, knowing it will be falling on deaf ears. I stand up when Jansen does and he comes over to me, putting his hands on my hips and grinning down at me.

"You realize he's totally going to spray all of them with the water."

"That's what I'm counting on. Dang kids are going to be the death of me." I mutter. "I'm sorry they are trying to hogtie you into—"

He stops me from talking by kissing my lips, his hands moving to cup my ass, and push me against him. I can feel his erection through his jeans and my body instantly softens to him. He pulls away a mere inch and our gazes lock.

"You don't hear me complaining one damn bit, Honey Girl," he whispers and before I can second guess myself, this time when our lips meet it's me who's doing the kissing.

I don't even have to think about it.

Jansen definitely has me hooked.

25

Jansen

I LOOK DOWN at the table leg I'm sculpting. It's been a long time since I've worked with wood and I'm missing the workshop I used to have. Still, it's not half bad and I think Ida Sue will like it. I bought some oak wood at the local sawmill and I'm using that. I'm hoping she'll see the significance. I stare at the wood in my hand, but my vision mostly tunes it out as my thoughts turn toward Ida Sue. Instead, it's her face I see.

I'm gone for that woman.

There's no other way to put it. I wouldn't have thought that was possible at my age, especially with my past.

But I am.

There's not a single thing that I don't like and admire about her. She's strong, probably the strongest woman I've ever met in my life. She's funny as hell when she comes out of her shell. She says and does the most off the wall things that it makes being around her... fun. Shit, I can't remember the last time I had fun. I'm not sure I have since I was a kid, fishing with my old man. I never realized it was missing in my life before now. But being around Ida Sue, being around her kids... I definitely realize it now.

I'm moving things slow with Ida Sue. She's been hurt a lot. I can see it, even if she hides it well. I'm fighting myself, because I want to just rush in and claim her as mine. I never thought I'd ever get married again. I want marriage with Ida Sue. I want her tied to me. I want to be cemented so deeply in her life that she'll never be able to see a future without me in it.

It seems that old dreams don't die, they just hibernate, because here I am at forty-four wanting a home and family again. Only this time the want is so much more... this time it just might be everything.

"Hey Jansen, what are you building?"

I turn to see Green standing at the door to the barn.

"It's a little late to be down this way, ain't it, son?"

"Probably, but I had too much on my mind. I needed to talk."

Green is young and he wouldn't understand. Chances are he'll never understand because he won't be my age without having a family or anyone to depend on him. But, the simple fact that he had crap on his mind and I'm the one he sought out to talk to, makes my chest grow tight. It might not have started out this way, but this family is mine. I feel it from the soles of my feet to the top of my head.

It took me a hell of a long time, but I finally found exactly where I belong.

"What's on your mind?" I ask him, clearing my throat because there's so much emotion running through me right now that I have to lock it down to contain it.

"Girls," he says with a sigh.

I hide my smile. He sounds so damn forlorn. I hate to break it to him, but the mystery that is women doesn't get any simpler with age.

"That's a broad category, Green."

"I asked Kayla to the homecoming dance."

"She turn you down?"

"Yeah."

My eyebrow cocks up at that news. I didn't expect it.

"How come?"

"She said she wasn't going to be a stand in for Cynthia."

"Well now. Let me ask you this, son. Would she have been?"

Green frowns. He looks down at the ground like he's sorting through everything in his mind.

"I don't think so. I mean, Cynthia and I have a history. I like her…. And… Can I tell you a secret, Jansen?"

"You can tell me anything, Son. Anything." Suddenly that emotion threatens again and I clear my throat.

"You won't tell anyone?"

"Whatever we talk about will always be between us, Green. I promise you that. The only time I would ever break that confidence is if whatever it is might cause you harm and then I'd tell your Momma."

His face stares straight at mine as if he's gauging what I say to determine if I'm being truthful. I hold his gaze and wait.

"Everyone thinks that Cyn and I have already had sex, but we haven't. I… well I haven't done that with anyone."

"Why do they think you have?"

"That's the thing. They just assumed it. I didn't tell them I didn't. I was going to, but Cynthia wouldn't let me. She said having the other cheerleaders thinking we were doing it, made them look up to her. So, I just played into it, instead. Now, everyone thinks we have."

I frown. "And this Cynthia wants it that way?"

"I don't know, girls are weird. Cynthia's older than I am. I mean I'll be sixteen this year. But, she's seventeen, so, maybe girls just think you have to have sex to be in a relationship. I probably should I guess. All my friends have."

"Boy, there's one thing you need to know about life. It moves fast enough on its own. You don't need to rush it along and never—and I mean never—do something you don't want to do because everyone else has."

"Well, Jansen, I mean it's not like I don't want to do it. I'm a guy and Cyn is hot. But…"

"But, what?"

"Sometimes I wonder if it's me she likes or the fact that I'm the star of the baseball team."

"Where does Kayla fit into all of this?"

"I thought it was me that she liked… but, it couldn't have been if she turned me down… Could it?"

"I don't know much about women, Green. They're a mystery to me, even at my age. I'd venture to say most men feel that way. But, I do know Kayla. That girl has a whole passel of issues about not feeling good enough and that stems from how hard she has it at home. I could see her worrying about not being good enough."

"But, she's pretty and sweet. Any guy would love to have her on his arm."

"You may see that, but I doubt Kayla does, son."

"That's sad."

"It is, but it's also a good reason for you not to ask Kayla out again, until you're sure how you feel."

"But…"

"Some girls are delicate. You can hurt them if you aren't careful, Green. A man never wants to hurt a woman. You do that and you're as low to the ground as a dog's belly."

"Some dogs are pretty tall," he jokes.

"Green—"

"Yeah, I get it, Jansen. Thanks for the advice. Maybe I should sort through my head before I take Kayla out."

"That might be a good idea," I agree.

"Besides there's always prom next year. Kayla would look hot in a prom dress."

I just shake my head. There's not much I can say to that.

"What are you making?"

"I'm making a kitchen table for your Momma for Valentine's."

"A kitchen table?"

"Yeah. You don't think she'll like it?"

"Jansen, maybe girls are a mystery to you because you don't understand what they like," he says.

"What do they like?" I ask, wondering if I should laugh, be offended or take notes.

"Not something like that," he says sagely, putting his hand on my arm. "Girls like chocolates and flowers for Valentine's Day. Trust me on this one, big guy. You get Mom a table for Valentine's and she's going to kick you to the curb."

"Well, I don't want that."

"None of us do. We like you and you make Mom laugh. She hasn't laughed in a long time."

I let that information settle inside of me.

I like it.

"I guess I should probably get some flowers to go on top of the table," I tell him, keeping my voice even and serious. I'll never tell him I was already going to give her flowers and a ring. He thinks he's helping me out and damn if I won't always let him believe that.

"That'd be a good idea. She likes lilies," he adds helpfully.

I grin. I guess he did help me out, after all.

"You want to help me on the table?" I ask, figuring he'd say no.

"Really? What do you want me to do?" he asks, surprising me, so I put him to work sanding the top I had forged together earlier.

It's going to be a huge table and damn sturdy, too. Hopefully, when I'm done, White, Gray, Green and the twins all could wrestle on it and maybe even throw Cyan into the mix and it'd still stand.

I just hope Ida Sue likes it.

26

Ida Sue

IT'S BEEN a hell of a day. I've been going since sun up and I haven't stopped. I delivered baked goods to several stores that sell them for me for a portion of the take. I delivered fifty custom cupcakes and four pies that the local sandwich shop ordered and then I cleaned three houses and Mrs. Fisher waved me down as I was leaving town and offered me cash if I helped at her diner, because the normal waitress got sick and had to go home. I was dead on my feet and I wanted to say no. I needed the money however, because Green's baseball is not cheap and neither are diapers for Mary, Maggie's school books, and the twins need new shoes...

The list seems to never end. Being a single parent is exhausting and a constant worry. I can't count the number of times I've woken up at four in the morning wondering if I had enough money coming in to make sure my kids had what they needed for the week. It's wearing me out. So, instead of coming home and having dinner with my children, seeing Jansen and relaxing, I called Maggie and asked if she'd watch the baby for me and told her to have the boys fend for themselves until I got home.

I hate this. I fucking hate it.

I feel like an absentee parent. I feel like I'm failing everyone, myself but mostly my children. Some look at me and they think I'm getting what I deserve for having so many children, others think I'm no better than a whore and never will be. Mostly I can write those people off, but some nights it gets to me. This is going to be one of those nights, maybe because I feel like they are right. But then, I never would have had so many children if I wasn't secure in my relationship with Orville. I forgot while he was alive what a bitch fate is and how it likes to sucker punch me.

I'm so tired that I could fall asleep, but I shake it off as the house comes into view. I've got to have enough energy to fix dinner for everyone, get Mary bathed and the kids tucked in. Then, I'll grab a glass of wine and collapse.

That plan changes when I see Jansen walking off the porch and making his way to the driveway.

"You're home late," Jansen says, opening my truck door as I shut the engine off.

"Don't I know it," I moan, sliding out of my seat onto the ground.

Jansen takes his strong arm and wraps it around me, pulling me into his body as he slams the truck door closed. I go willingly, too tired to even pull my head up to kiss him, instead settling for resting my head on his chest and having him hold me.

"You've got to quit working so hard, Lovey. You can't keep it up."

"I'll slow down soon. You're already helping with the ranch. We're on track to make profit again this month. I just need to catch up on things that have fallen behind and then—"

"Let me help, Ida Sue. I have money in the bank, I can—"

"Absolutely not."

"Why?"

"Because we're not at that point in our relationship. I will not take money from you, Jansen. If things work out and we're together and not just seeing each other on the side, then maybe it would be different. But—"

"You're a stubborn woman," he grumbles.

"I've been told that before," I agree, yawning.

"Have you eaten?"

"No. I'll make the kids something and—"

"They've already eaten, Lovey."

"They did?"

"Yep. I took care of it."

"You cook?"

"I ordered pizza. Does that count?" he says with a sweet smile and some of the burden of today somehow magically disappears.

"I think I love you," I exclaim, without thinking of how that sounds. I freeze in his arms and this funny look comes over his face. *Shit.* "I mean—"

I don't finish because his lips slam down on mine, robbing me of voice and breath. His kiss is urgent, his tongue unrelenting, his hand tightened to the point of pain in my hair and I love every moment of it. I hold onto him and let him take me where he wants, gasping when he pulls me up into his arms.

"Someday you're going to say those words to me, Lovey and you'll mean them," he vows, his voice hoarse and gravelly enough that it makes chills run through my entire body.

"Jansen," I murmur, trying to control my runaway heart. My legs are lying over his arm, his other at my back and his hand holding to my side as he carries me. "Where are we going?"

"I need some time alone with you."

Alright. I want that, too. But, I've already been an absentee mother most of the day...

"I need to make sure the kids get their homework finished and the baby—"

"I helped Green with his homework while Maggie bathed Mary. The others didn't really have any work and were playing videogames. We ate pizza and I cleaned the kitchen—which consisted of throwing away paper plates, empty boxes and bottles of soda. They're in their rooms now doing what kids do. You and I, Ida Sue, are going to spend some time alone."

"We are?"

"Definitely."

"Do I get to ask what we're doing?" I laugh, definitely feeling better than I did before I got out of the truck.

"First, you'll eat pizza."

"And then?"

"Then we'll do what adults do when they're alone."

"That sounds promising," I murmur, pressing a kiss against Jansen's shirt... *smiling*.

"God I hope so," Jansen says, his voice solid, strong... something you can hold on to.

Just like the man.

Maybe my luck has finally changed...

27

Jansen

"JANSEN, I mean, I thought we were going back to your office or the—"

"If the kids come looking for me, they aren't going to catch me with my hand down their Momma's pants, Lovey."

Her mouth opens, but she doesn't tell me to go to hell. Instead, she looks up at the big tree and the pieces of wood that have been nailed up it to make a ladder.

"Jansen, this is not a good idea. Let's go to—"

"You don't want me? Is that it?"

"Don't be stupid. We were just swappin' spit a minute ago. Despite what you may think, I don't let that many men stick their tongue in my mouth."

"Swappin' spit?" I bark, my head going back in shock. *I swear this woman…*

"Exactly."

"Such a romantic, you are, Lovey."

"Maybe I'd be romantic if you'd quit using dandelions for brains. You'd have to be dumb, blind and stupid to not know I want you."

"Then, what's the problem?"

"You want me to climb a ladder! And not even a real ladder, at that!"

"Lovey? Are you afraid of heights?"

"Of course not. Now, you're just ridiculous."

"Then, what——"

"I'm not scared, I'm more… anxious."

"Anxious?" I laugh, thinking that's probably the same.

"As a long-tailed cat in a room full of rocking chairs," she mumbles under her breath. "I ain't sure I can do this, Jansen."

"You can. I'll be right behind you."

"But…"

"Ida Sue, Honey Girl, look at me."

Slowly she brings her panicked face to look at me, her eyes wide. "Jansen——"

"I'm here with you. If you fall, I will catch you."

"But——"

"I'll always catch you, Lovey. Every. Damn. Time."

She doesn't say anything. She stares at me for a few minutes and then she slowly nods her head in agreement.

I should probably feel guilty for pushing her to do this. The truth is, it's not that high. She could fall out and probably be fine. I'm about to tell her not to worry about it, that I'll climb up and get the pizza and we'll go to my quarters, when she climbs the first step. I move in close behind her.

"If you let me fall, Jansen Reed, I'll kick you so hard you'll be walking around like there's a saddle horn stuck in your ass for days," she mutters.

I'd respond, but I'm doing my best to keep from laughing, so I just make sure she can feel my hand on her back as we climb the few short steps to the treehouse. I should be ashamed, because I can tell she's really afraid, but the entire time I get the view of her sweet ass in those tight jeans. I don't know a man alive who would want to pass up that show.

Once we make it inside she scoots over to where I have the

pizza sitting with a couple of sodas. I didn't plan in advance or I would have stopped in town and picked up some wine. This was the best I could do on short notice. I walk over to the small table the kids have to turn on the radio. I have to do it hunched over, because there's not enough room to stand.

"This damn thing needs to be taller, a man could get hunch-backed like this."

"It's tall enough for the kids," Ida Sue argues.

"Not for me." I click on the radio and the soft sounds of a country ballad fills the air.

"I don't think grown men are supposed to be in kids' play-houses, that's a little gross."

"Not if they're in it to seduce the kids' mother," I counter.

"Is that what you're doing?"

"If I say yes, are you going to take off running down the tree?"

"I'm still recovering from the climb up. I don't think I can handle a trip down just yet."

"So, you're saying I have you trapped here and at my mercy," I murmur going to sit beside her.

"I would be worried, but to be honest…"

"Yeah?" I ask, half listening as I drag my finger along the curve of her neck, moving upwards to her jawline.

"My lady balls are starting to turn blue from all the make out sessions we seem to have that never go anywhere."

My finger stills, my gaze going to her face.

"Lovey, if you have any kind of balls we might ought to call a halt to my plans for tonight."

"I wouldn't have figured you for the type of man to be afraid, Jansen Reed."

"Well, there's just some things a man can't overlook," I respond with a grin. I drop my finger back down her neck, following an imaginary line down her throat, across her stomach and only stopping when my hand is perched on the button of her jeans. "Still, you're one hell of a woman, Ida Sue. I should probably investigate before I just give up."

"I always did like a man with some stick-to-it-iveness," she replies, still smiling, but I can hear desire creeping deeper and deeper into her voice.

"I do like to please, Lovey," I admit, while undoing her jeans. The sound of the zipper slowly releasing makes my cock ache. Jesus, it feels like I've wanted this woman for years. It also feels like she's the only woman I've ever wanted in my life. Which solidifies my decision to give her a ring. I want her to wear my ring. I want everyone to know that she belongs to me.

At forty-four I finally found her.

The one.

I'm not about to let her get away.

28

Ida Sue

"I DO LIKE TO PLEASE, LOVEY."

My heart is beating out of my chest. I'm scared. I can admit that—at least to myself. I haven't been with a man in a long time. Even when Orville was alive, sex didn't happen that often and I was okay with that. I loved Orville, but it wasn't really a romantic love. With Jansen, my emotions are all messed in with my libido. If we do this, am I making a mistake? Will it ruin what we have? Can I even trust what we have?

I have all these questions and no real answers. But, I know that I want Jansen. I also know, that I want him enough to take this chance.

"What are you thinking about so hard, Honey Girl?" Jansen asks.

"Would you think I'm a fool, if I told you I was scared?"

"You don't have to be scared. I promise you, you can trust me."

"I think I can, but I'd be lying to both of us if I didn't admit that I have doubts."

"Then, I guess I'll just have to load those doubts away."

When he says that, his hands are busy sliding my pants down over my hips. His gaze never leaves mine, our eyes locked together, sharing this moment. It's been a long time since I was a virgin, but right now I feel like one all over again.

"I got you, Lovey. I promise, I'll always have you."

"Jansen…"

My voice breaks off in a gasp as I feel his fingers move softly against the lips of my pussy. They barely touch, just a gentle caress, and yet I can feel the wetness pool and slide against the tender folds in a way that he has to feel them against his fingers.

"You're safe with me, Lovey. I just want you to let yourself go. Can you do that? Just for tonight? Enjoy what I make you feel, let yourself fall and know that I'll be here to catch you."

My nails bite into his back as I hold onto him. I nod my head ever so slowly in agreement. He keeps his hand over my pussy, cupping the warmth there—but not moving.

With his free hand, he deftly pulls my t-shirt and bra up, exposing my breasts. A brief panic hits me because my breasts are not like they used to be. Having children and dancing that thin line close to forty has caused them to sag. I don't know what Jansen is used to in a woman, but I'm pretty sure it's not someone who has had nine children and breast fed each and every one of them. I've stopped breastfeeding Mary already, but my breasts are still tender, even though the milk is gone.

Will he be disappointed? Disgusted?!?!

"So damn beautiful, Ida Sue," he whispers, bending down.

His lips place a gentle kiss on my distended nipple. Then slowly, almost torturously, brings it into his mouth, sucking it against the roof of his mouth and then letting his tongue play. At the same time, his fingers brush across my other breast. The dual sensation sends hunger through my body. I cry out with need just as I feel him touch my clit.

His touch is petal soft, but it feels so wonderful that my hips rock upwards as I try to open myself up to him even more. He presses harder against my swollen clit, swirling in the wetness he finds there as he releases my nipple from his mouth. He blows against the wet skin sending goosebumps over the flesh. My body feels like a livewire that he's in control of.

"My beautiful Ida Sue. Soft and sweet as honey with enough fire to burn a man clean through. How in the hell did I get lucky enough to find you at this point in my life?" he murmurs, his eyes so dark they look like liquid.

"Jansen," I whisper, because his words smooth over my fear and leave me without words, other than his name.

"I'm going to make you come for me, baby. Make you come and then bury myself in you so I can feel you climax against my cock."

In all my years, sex has been an act, a mostly silent one. I've had good and I've had bad. With Orville, I could only describe it as good in its own way, but it was an act to show my love and gratitude. Jansen? Jansen is unlike anything I've ever experienced before. I love the way he talks to me, his voice deep and threaded with hunger. He doesn't hide his desire, and his words make me feel… *beautiful.*

Never.

I've never felt that way. Not since the day I was violated.

Not once.

It's silly to think that one man can heal a wound so deep that nothing has been able to even touch it, but right now that's what it feels like with Jansen.

Beautiful and safe.

29

Jansen

I SLIDE my fingers into her wet, heated depths. I can feel her walls flutter around me, opening, letting me in… trying to pull me in deeper. She's as skittish as a young foal and I don't want to scare her. I suspect that she's been hurt in the past. Something in her eyes gave that away. Now, I'm more convinced than ever that she has been. I want to go slow, to take my time and be gentle with her.

That need wars with the one that makes me want to bury myself so deep inside of her that she won't be able to walk without remembering how I felt between her legs. My cock is so hard that it's painful, the shaft pressed so tight against my jeans that I can feel the cold metal of the zipper pressing painfully.

"Hold your breast out for me, baby. Offer it up to me," I encourage, wanting her to be a part of our lovemaking, wanting her to give herself to me in every way.

Slowly she does, her face a deep pink—a mixture of hunger and shyness. I've never seen a woman more beautiful than she is right now. I suck the wanton, little nipple back into my mouth at the same time I begin moving my fingers in and out of her pussy. Her hips follow the slow but steady rhythm I set. I let my thumb graze against her clit. It's throbbing and so covered in her juices that I moan with the need to taste her.

"Look at me, baby," I command.

Her head is back, her eyes at half mast, her breathing ragged and she's completely lost to the sensations of her body. I drink it in, but I need her eyes on me.

"Ida Sue. Look at me," I repeat, making my voice harder, filled with authority.

Her head tilts upward to look at me, as I lift my hand from her body, her sweet little pussy trying to keep me inside. I tilt away from her body just enough, so I can bring the two fingers I had buried inside of her toward her upturned breast. I use them to paint her nipple, coating it in her juices and making it glisten, all while my gaze is locked on her face. She watches me, biting on her lip the entire time.

"Jansen…"

Before she can say anything else, I suck her nipple back into my mouth. I do it while I thrust my fingers back into her pussy. I keep my thumb pressed against her clit while I tunnel them in and out of her. I do it almost violently. There's nothing slow about the way I finger fuck her, nothing gentle about the way I ravish her breast with bruising force.

I can't go easy, not with the taste of her in my mouth, not while swallowing her sweet honey and taking it inside of me, and definitely not when I know she's marking me as hers so deeply that it will last a lifetime.

"Jansen," Ida Sue says again. Her fingers move through my hair, her nails scoring into my scalp and she pulls my head hungrily into her breast. "Don't stop," she gasps.

I groan, my mouth too full of her tit to reply, and I'm just unwilling to let it go.

"It feels so good, Jansen. Don't stop," she moans into my ear. I feel her lips move to the space where my neck and shoulder meet and then her teeth bite into me.

Jesus, fuck, that feels good.

"Can't stop, baby. I need inside of you. I want to make you come. I want to feel you come while I'm fucking you."

My voice is hoarse, guttural and full of a hunger so intense that it hurts to breathe. I pull away from her. Ida Sue is right there with me, grabbing her shirt and bra that I bunched up, getting ready to lift it over her head. I'm already undoing my pants, unable to wait another minute and then...

"Jansen? You up there?"

I hear Green call out to me from below.

"No..." I hear Ida Sue cry softly.

I want to cry with her.

"Fuck."

Ida Sue's head drops down as she pulls her bra and shirt back in place.

"Jansen! I came down to the barn to help you work on...

We're scrambling. I'm rebuttoning my pants, as Ida Sue tries to pull hers up just as Green pops up at the door.

"Ew! Gross! You're porking my mom!"

"Watch your mouth, Son," I growl.

"I'm going to have to burn my eyes out now," Green whines.

"Green, get out."

"Mom."

"I'll be in, in a bit. Get your ass down this tree and mind me before I give you something to whine about," she orders.

"Geez. Fine. I thought you said we weren't supposed to say ass," he mutters, moving back down the ladder.

"It's in the Bible, but I'll ask Jesus for forgiveness later, about the time I'm asking him to forgive me for setting your ass on fire and making it shine so bright the astronauts can see it from space, because you're backtalking me."

"I'm going, I'm going," he complains, before disappearing out of sight.

"Lovey—"

"Welcome to life with kids, Jansen," she sighs. "The damn

little cockblockers," she mutters laying back down on the pad I had on the floor.

"I guess the moment is over, huh?" I ask, moving to lie beside her, my balls throbbing.

"Yeah," she says, her eyes closed, her arm thrown haphazardly over her face. "Maybe this is a bad idea. I'm too old for a relation—"

I stop her with a kiss. It's quick and hard, but definitely effective. I pull back just enough so she can look into my eyes.

"If you think for one minute, Ida Sue Lucas, that I'm going to let you walk away from me after the sweet taste I just had of you, you better damn well think again."

"Jansen—"

"I'm not letting you go. I want you, *all* of you. I even want your crazy kids. That's not going to change, Honey Girl."

She watches me closely, her eyes appraising me. I feel like I'm holding my breath. I was serious when I told her that I wasn't giving her up, but it sure as hell would make things easier if she didn't fight me on it. Her hand comes up and rests on the side of my face.

"You could find a woman it'd be simpler to have something with, Jansen," she says gently.

"I'd rather have something with a woman that I know was worth all the bullshit that goes along with a relationship, Lovey."

"All the bullshit?" she questions with a smile.

"You're not walking away from me, Ida Sue. I won't let you."

"I should. It'd be easier for both of us."

"I don't like easy. Give me complicated any day of the week and twice on Sunday if that means it's you I'm kissing and you who I'm buried deep inside of when the morning sun comes up."

"What am I going to do with you Jansen Reed?"

"Keep me."

"I don't suppose you're giving me a choice," she says, her head dropping down.

I wrap her up in my arms, kissing the top of her head.

"Now you're starting to understand," I murmur softly against her hair.

I hold her like that. I don't know how long. Long enough for the ache of unfulfilled need to leave us both. Long enough to recognize that after all this time I've finally fallen in love.

For the last time in my life.

30

Jansen

"AND WHAT ARE YOU DOING?"

I turn to see Ida Sue grinning at me. She has her hair pulled up today and she's wearing a soft yellow dress, holding a sleeping Mary in her arms. She's enough to take a man's breath.

"Well, it's Saturday and I finished riding the fence lines, so I thought I'd rope the boys into helping me on a project."

"What kind of project?"

She has a saucy grin when she asks me that. If I wasn't surrounded by all of her kids, I'd tackle her to the ground. It's been barely two days since our evening in the treehouse, but it feels like forever. If I don't have her soon, I'm going to go insane.

"I have this girlfriend who is afraid of heights, so the boys and I have decided to build a new playhouse."

"It's a clubhouse, Jansen," Black complains.

"Yeah man, you're messing with our street cred calling it a playhouse," Green adds.

"Petal has more street cred than you do, dumbass," Blue mutters.

"Mom, Blue called me a dumbass," Green whines.

126

"That's because you're being one, dear," Ida Sue answers, giving me a wink.

"Yeah, you're being one!"

"Cyan, stop it before I wash your mouth out with soap."

"Yeah, stop," Green says, pushing his brother.

"How about all of you stop and run into the house and get us some waters while I talk to your mom?"

"Yeah, let's go. They're probably going to get all kissy-faced," Green mutters, the first one to run away. Ida Sue holds her head down.

"Mom and Jansen sitting in a tree. K-I-S-S-I-N-G," Cyan sing-songs, following the rest of his brothers in the house.

"It's amazing how that boy can spell to irritate the piss out of me, but flunk his tests in school that ask him to spell the word box," she says with a sigh.

I laugh.

"Where are you two headed today?"

"I was going to see if you wanted to go into town with me. I wanted to take Mary and find some shoes. She's outgrown her last pair and she needs some to support her feet now that she's walking so much."

"She sure is getting big, she barely fits in your arms now."

"Don't I know it? This child is a chunk. Really, I was just hoping to spend some time with you. You look busy, though. Why are you building a playhouse?"

"Because you're afraid of heights."

"I'm not following."

I wipe my hands on my pant legs and reach out and take Mary. Even over the sweat and heat of the day, I smell her little baby smell and it wraps around my heart. Ida Sue lets her go with a sigh.

"Shew, she was starting to break my arms. Now tell me what you're talking about."

"You're afraid of heights. What happens if one of the kids get up in that tree and needs you? And what about little Petal?

She's starting to go up in there more and more. It's not that high up, but she could still get hurt. Plus, there are a lot of boards on that thing that need replaced. It's not entirely safe."

"I know. It's just nothing I've been able to fix on my own."

"So, I'm fixing it for you."

"You're fixing the treehouse by building a playhouse?" she laughs.

"I'm going to tear the treehouse down and use the good wood, along with what I have to build a bigger playhouse for the kids. That way everyone is happy and you aren't worrying yourself to death."

"And the boys agreed to this?"

"I can be very persuasive," I brag and I'm rewarded with Ida Sue's blush.

"You don't have to tell me twice, Jansen Reed. Trust me, I already know."

"Then, you might like to know that I'm making it big enough that you and I can stand up in it."

"Umm… okay?"

"That way when I do get you to myself again, we don't have to waste time. I'll just push you up against the wall and take you," I tell her, my voice dropping down.

I watch her eyes dilate, her face fill with heat and I can read the hunger on her body clearly—maybe because it mirrors my own.

"You better make it extra sturdy then, Jansen."

"Already working on it, Lovey."

"Good," she says leaning in to kiss me.

"Mom! Jansen! Come quick!"

Both of us freeze and turn to look at Maggie who is running toward us with panic in her voice. Kayla and Petal are running just behind her. I hand the baby back and walk to them, Ida Sue close on my heels.

"What's wrong girls?"

"We were walking out by the creekbank, close to the Mighty

128

Oak," Maggie says, using the nickname that everyone calls the oak tree that now holds mine and Ida Sue's initials.

"We were looking at the new calves in the pasture and there's this gunky black stuff bubbling in their pond. They can't drink that, Jansen! It will make them sick!" Kayla adds, out of breath.

"I don't want the baby cows to die, Jansen," Petal cries.

"They won't die, baby," I tell her leaning down to wipe a couple of her tears away. "I better saddle up Duke and see what's going on," I add.

"Maggie, you take Mary. Jansen and I will take the truck and see what's going on."

"Ida Sue—"

"It'll be quicker and besides you might need my help."

"But your dress, you might stain it—"

"There are other dresses. Let's get going. Those calves put food on our table. Maybe someday they might even provide a table," she jokes, handing the baby over to Maggie.

I grin. I have her table done. I just need to put the final varnish on the benches and then I'll show her. I wish it was already Valentine's Day, because I really want to show her now.

I take her hand and we head out towards the shed on the side of the barn.

Soon, I can give her the table and the ring.

I just hope she says yes…

31

Jansen

"YOU MADE THIS?" Gray asks as him and White walk into the barracks where I've been staying. Tomorrow is Valentine's Day and I find myself getting nervous. Things have been crazy since Kayla and Maggie discovered oil was bubbling up by where I had put in some fence posts the day before. I'm not expecting much from it. I suspect I tapped into an old line that was run through the pasture while Orville was alive. Ida Sue doesn't have any idea about that kind of thing. Still, it is all that's been on everyone's minds here, including Ida Sue's. Which means, I haven't had a chance to talk to her alone—at least about us. I think we're on the same page, but I would have liked a little more time with her before popping the question tomorrow.

I guess in some ways I might be jumping the gun kind of quick. The thing is, it doesn't feel quick to me. I've spent most of my life alone, feeling like I had nothing in this world that mattered. The moment I saw Ida Sue my attention was captured. After talking to her, I felt... *centered*. Spending time with her, kissing her, laughing with her, watching her with her children and a million other little things have made it clear that Ida Sue is my future.

I'm forty-four and I don't want to waste another moment of my life. I want to begin our lives together.

I can only hope Ida Sue feels the same.

"Yeah. Do you think your Momma will like it?" I ask, hoping I'm hiding my nerves, at least a little. I made a huge table. It's not anything special. Without my work shop, I couldn't put a lot of special touches on it. I did a dark stain and made sure it was big enough to fit a family the size of this one and could even fit a little more as the kids get older and have families of their own. I carved small flowers into the legs. Basically, it was small flowers climbing up the legs on a vine. There's a lotus flower, a magnolia blossom and a marigold. I even added in a buttercup, because it's looking more and more like little Kayla will end up living here full time. Her mother is extremely sick, and Kayla's stepfather shows zero interest in the little thing.

At the top of each leg, I've carved a lily and I colored it a soft pink which reminds me of Ida Sue. I'm hoping she likes it, that she understands what I'm saying with the table. Most of all I hope that she understands that she means everything to me. I tried to show her with this gift.

I took special care with each of the flowers and stained each a different color. Pale black, soft blue, a white wash, a light green, and a medium gray. Cyan was the tricky son to pin down. I'm not even going to lie, I had no idea what that color was. When I looked it up and discovered it was a mixture of green and blue, I had a hell of a time getting it to turn out. I finally got close I think. The sales lady called the stain a silky teal. I don't know about any of that, but it's pretty and blended in well with the others.

Because I was crunched for time and spent way too much making the flowers and colors mean something, I ended up just making large benches instead of chairs. Each bench has the letter I engraved in the wood. I started to add a J, but I didn't want to overstep.

"Damn Jansen, this is beautiful. You built this in just a couple of weeks?"

"Yeah. I used to do a lot of wood working. It came pretty easy," I tell them, underplaying it. The truth is, I worked nonstop. I'd get up two hours early every morning and work before I went out on the ranch and checked the fields and the pastures. Then, I'd come back after dinner and I'd work until I was literally falling asleep. If it wasn't for Green's help, I'm still not sure I would have gotten it done.

"Mom will love it," White says, looking at me strange.

"What?" I ask, knowing what's coming next.

"When you called last night and asked to talk to me and Gray alone, I won't lie Jansen. I thought maybe you were planning on leaving."

"We didn't want that—just for the record," Gray adds.

"We like you and for the first time since we can remember, Mom is laughing freely."

"She was happy with Orville," I tell them, needing to make it clear that I'm not trying to replace the man who became their father.

"She was happy, but she worried. She never let herself relax, even as a child I can remember that. Mom always worried she wasn't good enough," White says. "I even heard them talking about it once. It didn't matter what Orville said, Mom just felt she caused Orville problems."

"This town sucks ass. They talked about her all the time and she hated that Orville had to hear it," Gray grumbles, obviously bitter.

"Your mother is the strongest person I've ever met in my life boys. She's special."

"You love her," White says.

"I do. It's happened quick, but that doesn't change things at all. Which is why I wanted to talk to you. I..." I break off, rubbing the back of my neck and feeling a little out of my depth. "I want to get your blessing."

"Our blessing?" Gray asks, but White smiles. He already knows what I want.

"I'm planning on marrying your Momma. I'm from another time, I know, but I wouldn't feel right without asking you first."

"What are you going to do if we say no?" White asks.

"Ask her anyway," I laugh. "But, I sure would feel better knowing I'm asking with you two on my side," I add honestly.

They both look at me and for once their faces are completely solemn. I start to worry, but then they both begin to smile.

"Can't think of a man I'd rather have as a stepdad," Gray says, slapping me on the shoulder and giving me a hug.

"Do I have to call you Dad?" White smirks.

"You can call me anything you want, as long as you're okay with me marrying your Mom."

"Welcome to the family, Jansen," he says and for the first time since the girls found that damn oil bubbling up in the field, I breathe a little easier.

Now if Ida Sue just says yes…

I FEEL like a damned cat on a hot tin roof. I'm jumping around from place to place. I can't concentrate at all. The house is way too quiet, too, and that doesn't help. If you add in the fact that Jansen and I have a date tonight... It's a wonder I'm still standing.

I look in the mirror for the hundredth time. I left my hair down and brushed it until it shined. I started to curl it, do something to make it look different, but I stopped myself. Jansen seems to like me. He's seen me when I've looked like death warmed over. I'm too old of a dog to try and learn new tricks—even for him. So, I kept my hair the way I prefer to wear it. I did put on makeup and the pink dress he seems to love. I've worn it a few times and each time I've noticed his eyes stay on me a little longer, his caresses are a little more intense and his voice sounds more graveled, threaded with need when he tells me I look pretty. It's been a while, but I think those are all very clear signs. They make me feel pretty anyway.

With one last glance, wishing my push up bra pushed my girls up a little higher, I give a defeated sigh and go and check on Mary. She went down about thirty minutes ago, which is earlier than normal. That will probably mean I'll be up with a wide awake two-year-old late tonight, which is bad. I let her go to sleep though, because it also means a sleeping toddler now might actually get me laid tonight. I miss sex. I haven't had it since Mary was conceived actually. There's a good chance I have cobwebs growing up in there and having a house full of kids makes using anything battery operated useless. I swear their little ears hear *everything*.

That doesn't mean the thought of having sex with Jansen doesn't scare me to death. *It does.* I'm just hoping that I can finagle it to where we're in my room in the dark. The dark hides a multitude of sins and the good Lord knows that my body has a lot of things that need hidden.

I head downstairs and walk into the kitchen and jump when I see Jansen, White, Gray and Green all standing in a line. The boys grinning like a bunch of roosters that just snuck into the hen house—which is never a good thing—and Jansen standing there looking nervous as hell.

"What's going on?" I ask, eyeing them all closely.

"Nothing, Mom. Just sitting here shooting the shit with Jansen," White says, slapping his hand on Jansen's shoulder.

"Let me ask you boys something."

"What's that, Mom?"

"Do I look any different than I did yesterday, White? Because I didn't buy bullshit when you tried to sell it to me then, either."

"Uh-oh." I hear Green mumble under his breath and that just proves that at least one of my sons has a few brain cells left.

"Uh… Well you look prettier," he says.

"You do look pretty, Mom," Gray agrees.

"Definitely," Green adds—way too cheerfully.

"Pretty as a picture," Jansen says walking to me. The boys shuffle behind him and I should pay attention to them, but my gaze is locked on the man smiling down at me.

"Stop distracting me," I mumble. "My boys are up to something."

"Nothing bad, I promise you, Honey Girl."

"You're in on it too."

"A man just needs to surprise his woman sometimes, Ida Sue. That's all. How about you and I go outside and take a walk for a bit?"

"Mary is sleeping."

"Then we'll go outside on the porch and sit in the old swing. You've got that baby monitor, right?"

"Yeah."

"Then we'll grab it."

"But the boys," I mumble trying to look over Jansen's shoulder.

"We're going to be heading out, Mom. We're spending the night at White's buddy Davis's house," Gray says.

"All three of you?" I ask, even as Jansen puts his arm around me and practically forces me to walk into the living room.

"Yep. We'll just finish moving those things in for you, Jansen."

"Sounds good boys. Appreciate your help."

"Anytime," they chime in and I give up trying to look behind me. It's clear that Jansen isn't going to let that happen.

"What are they moving in?"

"It's a surprise."

"Seems like tonight has a lot of surprises," I respond, picking up the baby monitor off the coffee table and taking it outside with us.

"You got something against surprises, Lovey?"

"I usually like to be prepared."

We sit down on the swing together and Jansen takes the monitor and puts it on the ground by our feet. Then, he pulls me into his arms, lifting me so that I'm mostly sitting on his lap.

"That's better," he says with a satisfied grin.

I wiggle just a little to get comfortable and I can feel the hard ridge of his cock under my ass.

"Keep doing that, Ida Sue and the only surprise you'll be

getting is me taking you upstairs and giving you the hardest fucking you've ever had in your life," he growls.

"I'd be okay with that."

"Ida Sue."

"I assume your surprise is the reason all of my children are out for the night."

"All of them?"

"Even Petal. Apparently, my friend Leddie wanted to bake cookies with a little girl and her daughter Meadow is getting too old to enjoy it. So, she mysteriously wanted to borrow Petal for the night. Would you know anything about that?"

"Why would I know about that?"

"Now that's the million-dollar question, isn't it?"

"Does this mean I have you alone tonight?"

"With the exception of Mary, yes."

"You have really good kids, Ida Sue."

"They are, and a whole lot of sneaky. I'm beginning to think you have some of that in you too, Jansen Reed."

"Maybe a dash. Are you going to make a man beg for a kiss, or what?"

"Would you beg?" I laugh.

"For you, baby? Every damn time."

He says that with such intensity on his face, what can I do other than kiss him? Which is exactly what I do.

I think I might love Jansen Reed.

Lord help me. Lord help us both. Love never works out for me. And I've never felt for anyone the way I feel about Jansen.

Which means when this falls apart, it just might kill me.

And that's terrifying.

33

Jansen

THERE'S one thing I can say about Ida Sue Lucas. Okay there's lots of things, but right now all I can think is that she can kiss. She kisses better than a woman ought to have a right to. She's ruined me for any other woman and that's the damn truth. If I hadn't already decided to marry her the kiss she just gave me would have definitely made my mind up for me.

We break apart, both of us breathing hard. I've unbuttoned the top of her dress and pushed my hand inside, palming her breast, and I don't even know how that happened. I need to get control, but with my hand full of her breast, her ass pushing and grinding down against my hard cock and the taste of her kiss, I don't know if that's possible.

"I had plans, Lovey, but I have to have you," I growl into her ear. I suck the lobe in my mouth, biting down on it and then soothing it with my tongue.

"Plans can wait. Let's go upstairs," she murmurs.

She barely has the words out before I have her in my arms and I'm carrying her back into the house. She's unbuttoning my shirt, placing small kisses with each inch of skin that she reveals.

"Fuck, woman," I growl when her sweet little tongue laps against my nipple.

"I love that you have hair on your chest, Jansen. I love the way it feels when I rub my face against it. I like it almost as much as when I make you say fuck…"

"Make me say it?" I grin, turning the corner to get to the stairs.

"You come off as very straight and narrow, Jansen. You could pass for a country preacher," she says. And I stop in my tracks, pulling back to look at her.

"The fuck you say?"

"There you go again. When you say fuck it's like the devil himself sets my body on fire, angels weep and the only way the hunger inside of me can be quenched is if you cover me in your holy water."

"Don't think I have any holy water, Lovey," I laugh, looking down at this woman that I love more than life and thinking she might be as pretty as she is crazy. I like both. She brings a lightness into my life that has never been there before.

"We'll improvise. I think you might have something even better," she says, her tongue moving along her bottom lip. I'm so hypnotized by watching that, I miss her hand moving down to massage the hard outline of my cock in my jeans. There can be no missing what she means.

"*Fuck*, woman. You grab hold of my *fucking* cock like that one more time, I'm going to *fuck* you so hard you won't be able to walk for *fucking* days."

I watch as her eyes dilate, her breathing harsher and realize she's telling the truth. She loves it when I say the word fuck. That's good information to have and I'll make sure to use it to my advantage.

I just have to get her upstairs first.

"Jansen?" I stop on the first stair.

"Yeah, baby?"

"What is that?" she asks, her voice so soft and quiet that I almost don't hear it. That's when I notice she's staring in the direction of the kitchen… *specifically the table.*

I slowly let her slide down my body so she's standing beside me, sudden nerves overtaking my hunger for her body. I think she'll like the table. I'm praying she does. Still, there's a chance she won't. There's a larger chance that she won't understand the message I'm trying to give her.

There's also the fact that my entire future is hinging on what happens here tonight.

"I..." I clear my throat. "...Made you something for Valentine's Day."

"A table." She walks toward it, her voice so quiet that it's hard to hear and I can't read the emotion in it to know what she's thinking.

"Lovey—"

"You made me a table, Jansen."

Now, I'm really starting to worry. Maybe her boy was right. I rub the back of my neck. "I got you some flowers too," I tell her, clumsily moving the vase of lilies and daisies up from the center of the table.

"It's huge," she continues to murmur.

"You have a big family, Ida Sue."

She puts her hand on the top of it and carefully slides it around. Her head is down, so I can't really see what's going on in her head. "You made me a table." Her voice is still soft and I think there's a touch of wonder in it.

Maybe she does like it.

She sits down on the bench and I start to relax a little. She wouldn't have done that if she didn't like it... *Right?*

"You made me a table."

"Ida Sue..."

She finally turns to the side and looks at me. There are tears in her eyes and the sight of them hits me wrong—a million times wrong.

"Ida Sue, Lovey, you don't have to keep the table. I just was trying to—"

"In my whole life, Jansen, no one has ever bothered to do anything like this for me."

"Ida Sue—"

"You used oak."

"You admired the wood for being strong, thought it felt like protection over your family and land. I couldn't use anything else after hearing you talk about that old oak tree."

"You made me a table and you listened to me," she says.

"Lovey, you're going to have to let me in that brain of yours," I finally tell her. I kneel down on the floor in front of her, using my thumb to brush away the tears on her face. She shifts a little on the bench and her hand moves over the letter I that is engraved deep in the wood.

"You put my initial on it."

"You're the foundation of the family, Ida Sue. Your children adore you. You'd give the world to see them happy."

"You know me," she whispers.

"Ida Sue—"

"I want your initial under mine, Jansen."

"Ida Sue. This table was for you and your kids, I'm just—"

"If I'm the foundation of this family, like you say then, you are *my* foundation, Jansen. I want your initial there."

Now, it's my turn to be speechless. I look in her face and I let my hands cup the side of her face, pushing them under her hair.

"I'll put it on there."

"I love you, Jansen Reed."

Something clicks into place with those words. Something I've been missing since the day I was born.

"I love you, Ida Sue Lucas." I kiss her then. A slow kiss, full of all of the emotion inside of me, a kiss that promises her that I'll be with her forever.

A kiss to tell her that I'm not going anywhere.

A kiss that says I'm finally home.

34

Ida Sue

I'VE SQUATTED down to see the legs of the table. They're beautiful, so much more than I ever would have imagined. Jansen has shown me the flowers and colors on the legs and I know I've not spoken or responded, but I honestly haven't been able to form the words. To know he took the time to hand carve and stain something so individual so that everyone in my heart was represented... Orville was good to me. I loved him for being an anchor when I was horribly lost. But, as good as he was, it would have never occurred to him to do something for me... just for me. We didn't have that kind of a relationship. Our lives centered around the kids and that was fine.

But this...

My finger moves over the lily. It looks delicate and pink even though it's carved into the wood. I wet my lips and swallow down the emotion that surges inside of me.

"Why did you put the lily on here, Jansen?" I finally ask, standing up.

"White and I had a talk while he was in. When I showed him the table, I was originally going to put an I on each of the legs. Then, he told me about your name Peace Lily.

"Jansen, I'm not——"

"It's a part of you. It's who you were before you were hurt, Ida Sue."

"How do you know I was hurt?" I ask, my heart beating wildly in my chest.

"Because that's part of who you are now, too. I might not know the whole story, but I can see it. Someday you can tell me the whole story."

"I don't think——"

"When you're ready you will. I don't think you get this, Sweetheart, but I'm not going anywhere. I'm staying right here with you," he vows, brushing my hair away from my face. My tears, I wasn't even aware I was still crying, he sweeps away on his thumb. "I'm here until you tell me to go," he adds.

It feels like a promise and one I'm desperate to believe.

"What if I keep you?" I'm trembling even as I ask the question, but I have to ask it.

"I'm praying you do, Darlin'. Fuck me, I'm really praying you do," he murmurs, his lips claim mine, and while we're kissing I feel his hands against my ass, pressing me into him and the hard ridge of his cock feels heated against my stomach.

He lifts me up, his lips never leaving mine and I immediately wrap my arms and legs around him, holding on. My ass hits the table and he lowers me on it, pulling away from our kiss. We look at each other, both of us breathing hard. He pulls his shirt open, and if it didn't have snaps, I'm sure buttons would have gone flying. I rub my lips together, watching as he reveals his body to me—*just waiting.*

He kicks his boots off next and still I can do nothing but watch, totally hypnotized by him. I watch as his face softens from the harshness of desire and he grins at me.

"You've got too many clothes on, Darlin'."

I've noticed Jansen has used a lot of pet names with me, but I think "Darlin'" might be my favorite.

"I'm just enjoying the show, Cowboy. Just enjoying the show." I'm grinning as I respond, the smile stops as my mouth falls open with a soft whimper when he unzips his pants, pushes them down over his hips.

His cock is dark, thick, with a broad head and long in a way I've not seen. I squirm on the table, just taking it in.

"Ida Sue?"

"Yeah," I ask, my voice sounding breathless, my gaze glued on his cock as he takes it in his hand and strokes.

"My eyes are up here, Darlin'."

"Yeah," I say again, mostly ignoring him, unable to take my eyes from his cock.

His laughter finally hits me and I eventually look up at his face.

"Undress, Ida Sue," he says, his eyes crinkled with happiness.

It feels like my heart swells in that moment, overfilling in a way I've never experienced.

But, I know that it's good.

"UH... MAYBE WE COULD MOVE UPSTAIRS."

I look at her and smile.

"I want you here, Lovey. Right here on this table."

"I..."

"Is it too soon?"

"Hell no."

"Then what's the problem, Darlin'?"

"I really like it when you call me, Darlin'."

"Ida Sue," I warn with a laugh. This woman is giving me whiplash.

"Can we turn the lights out?"

"Why would I do that?"

"Jansen... I'm almost forty."

"And I'm past that. What does that have to do with a damn thing?"

"I've had nine kids, Jan."

"Ida Sue," I respond with a sigh.

"Having a child does things to your body," she mumbles, blushing a deep red.

"Ida Sue, don't you think I know that?"

"I've only had clothes on when we've fooled around."

"Darlin'—"

"Clothes hide a multitude of sins," she mutters. "I just think it'd be better with the lights off at least for a little while."

"Ida Sue. I'm forty-four. I don't make a habit of sleeping with women who aren't my age, or at least close to it. Do you think I haven't seen a woman's body before and been able to appreciate it?"

She frowns at me, her eyes narrowing.

"I'd rather not hear about the women before me that you've stuck your sausage into, Jan, or I might determine I'm a vegetarian."

"Why is it when I'm around you I don't know whether to kiss you or spank your ass, Ida Sue?"

"I don't remember spanking being on the table."

"It will be eventually. For now, it's you on the table, with the lights on, and if you have any doubts on how I like your body, I'm going to fuck those out of you."

"You said fuck again."

Some of the nervousness has left her face now and she's smiling. Her face is flushed.

"Are you going to take that dress off?" I ask.

"What if I told you I have granny panties on under this dress?"

"I'd tell you the sight of granny panties on you makes my cock weep with joy."

Her mouth drops into an 'O' shape, and then she laughs.

"What if I told you I don't have any panties on?"

"Then, I'd tell you the good Lord above has answered my prayers and my cock would weep with joy," I tell her, my voice dropping down in tone as I reach behind her and deftly unzip her dress.

"So basically, no matter what, your cock is going to be wet." She stares at me, licking along the seam of her lips and pulling her arms out of her sleeves. Once she does that she clasps the top of her dress against her chest.

146

"Definitely wet, Darlin'."

"Jan—"

"Wet from the root…" I murmur softly into her ear as I gather her dress at the hemline and slowly push it upwards. "… to the tip," I finish, biting teasingly on her earlobe. Then, I continue pulling the dress up past her hips. I have to stop at her waistline because she's clutching it so tightly.

"Jan, I really do have a nice soft bed…"

"We'll try it out later."

"Why later?" she asks, remaining stubborn.

"Because right now I want my woman on this table, naked, open for me and begging me to go deeper."

"I don't normally beg," she warns me and that makes me grin.

"You will," I promise her just as I pull hard and lift the dress over her head.

That's the moment I discover that she wasn't actually wearing granny panties. She didn't have panties on at all. And the lips of her pussy are glistening with her juices.

I'm definitely going to make sure she begs me to go deeper and when I'm done, she'll never doubt how much her body turns me on.

Never.

36

Ida Sue

SWEET LORD, Jansen could sweet talk a nun out of giving up her chastity. I close my eyes tightly, so tight that it's almost painful. I don't want to see the disappointment on his face when he takes in the stretchmarks around my stomach and arms. I admit it's shameful. I should have a stronger backbone, but I can't stand to see disappointment in Jansen's eyes.

I just can't.

I wait and nothing happens. I haven't heard his footsteps, or I'd be even more panicked thinking he had left the room. My heart is thumping in my chest so hard it's echoing in my ears.

It feels like I've been like this, eyes squeezed shut, for at least an hour, even if it has been a minute or two.

Then, I squeak a soft gasp out when I feel Jansen's lips against the wet lips of my pussy. My eyes spring open immediately.

"Jansen…"

"You're fucking beautiful, Lovey. Never seen anything prettier."

"You don't have to say that—"

"And I've never tasted anything better in my life," he growls as his hand cups my pussy.

"How you could even think I'd find you anything but beautiful, Ida Sue, I don't understand. I've seen you before in the treehouse, remember? Did I act like I didn't love everything about you then?"

"Well, I mostly kept my clothes on and we worked around them."

"I remember you feeding me your breast, my fingers buried in your sweet pussy and—"

"I just..."

"Just what, Lovey?" he asks.

My eyes go wide when he sits on the bench he made for the table. I try to close my legs, but he doesn't let me. Instead, he puts one leg on each of his shoulders, leaving me completely open and angled for his mouth.

"I wanted to be perfect for you..." I realize I sound silly and I sigh, feeling a little foolish.

"Lean on your elbows so you're looking at me, Ida Sue," he orders.

I do as he asks. He's seeing parts of me that kind of make it impossible to worry anymore. He either likes it or he doesn't at this point. His fingers graze over the lips of my pussy, barely touching it, teasing me more than anything and it's enough to cause my body to shiver in reaction.

I grow wetter just from the way he's looking at me, barely touching me. Maybe it should embarrass me, being open to him like this, growing so wet that my juices slide against his fingers, but suddenly all of my worries fade and all I want is for him to take me, to make this delicious ache he created... *stop*.

He bends down, flattening his tongue against my pussy and licking, gathering up my desire and taking it into his mouth. My eyes flutter closed. It's still barely a touch, but it, along with the wet heat of his tongue, is enough to make my body shudder with need. Then, I feel his tongue slide between my lips and I moan because it feels so good. He pulls apart my lips so that I'm open to him and when I look at him again, Jansen is staring down at my exposed pussy.

"I love your body Ida Sue. I love everything about it."

"Jansen, please…"

"I especially love that you're giving it to me. You are, right Darlin'?"

"I am?"

I gasp as he stops talking and his tongue slides against my throbbing clit. It curls around it somehow and then he's sucking on it, pulling it between his lips, as his fingers thrust into me. He releases me with a popping noise, his fingers deep inside of me. I feel his thumb pressing against my swollen clit thrusting back and forth as he finger fucks me.

"Say it, Ida Sue. Tell me that you're giving me your body. That it's mine to keep," he says, his voice harsh, full of hunger and so raspy that it makes me want to purr.

He begins placing small kisses around my clit, always so close—but, never touching it. His fingers still slide in and out of me, fucking me slow and steady. I squirm needing his attention back at my clit and needing it in a way that I've never needed anything in my entire life before.

"Tell me, Lovey. I need to hear it," he says, this time kissing downward to my inner thighs, his teeth nipping and dragging across my skin.

I'm squirming in his hands, having a hard time concentrating and needing him to stop playing with me. I try to focus, knowing it's important to give him what he wants, but I just need him to come back to my clit.

"Tell me, Lovey," he says again, kissing his way back up. His fingers stop moving inside of me. They're buried deep and I squeeze my muscles to try and ride them, but I can't get what I need.

"Jan, honey, I need you to give me more," I beg and I don't care that I do sound like I'm whining.

He's killing me.

"I need the words, Lovey," he says softly as he blows air against my clit.

Sweet Jesus…

"I…"

His fingers stretch inside of me as he kisses the top of my clit, then he sucks it into his mouth, his teeth biting down as his tongue tortures it.

And then he stops.

"Ida Sue…" he says, his voice warning.

I'm going mindless. I've never been so worked up and if he doesn't stop torturing me and just give me what I want…. *I may have to kill him.*

"Jan…" I whimper.

"Give me the words, and I'll make this pretty little pussy come all over my face," he promises.

I'm breathing hard, and slowly going out of my mind, when he curls his fingers inside of me, and moves the pads of them back and forth on the upper wall of my vagina. Perspiration breaks out over my body, I tremble, feeling a climax that is simmering just out of reach. My entire life I've heard of the G-spot and where it's located, but I've never had a man find it. Jansen not only can find it, he seems to know where it is without searching.

Words… he needs words… I need to remember what he wants me to say.

At this point I'd say anything if he just never stops.

If he just makes me come.

"I'm giving you my body, Jansen," I cry, proud of myself for remembering, when I feel a finger press against the tight ring of muscle at my ass.

"That's my woman," he praises, sucking my clit back in his mouth while his fingers begin moving inside of me again and his thumb pushes against my ass.

"Come for me, Darlin'. Come for me," he murmurs, as my

clit slides from his mouth and his tongue begins lapping against it.

"Jansen," I cry, the orgasm so huge that I'm afraid to let it go now. It feels like it might destroy me.

"Come for me, Lovey," he croons. "Give me all that sweet juice you have inside, Honey Girl."

There's a part of me trying to hold it back. A little out of fear and also because I want to make it last, but with Jansen's fingers barreling in and out of me, I can't stop myself. The orgasm speeds through me, my legs tighten against him and I come, giving him everything I have.

37

Jansen

"THAT'S a damn fine table you made, Jan."

Ida Sue laughs into my side, her arms around me, squeezing me to her as her leg lays over mine. I've got her head on my shoulder, her hair fanned out over it and I'm gently stroking her arm. Her comment would make me smile, but I haven't stopped smiling, not since the moment I made her come and especially not afterwards when I slid my cock deep inside of her and we came together.

We ended up making a sandwich instead of going out. Not what I had planned, but this way we could let Mary sleep, and if I'm honest, I liked it better and I think Ida Sue did too. Mary woke up and I played with her and helped Ida Sue get her down for the night. I've not been around many babies, but little Mary seemed to take to me and Ida Sue didn't yank her out of my hands, so I figure I did okay.

Now it's hours later and Ida Sue and I should be asleep, but I don't want to sleep. Part of me is afraid that if I fall asleep, I'll wake up alone and this—all of this—will be a dream. When a man suddenly has everything he ever wanted in his arms, I'm finding that it makes you afraid it's not real.

"Glad you like it, Lovey," I murmur into her hair, kissing her there and giving her a squeeze.

"You've gone quiet."

"Just thinking that tonight might be the single greatest night in my life."

Maybe I should try to play it cool, hold myself back, but that's not who I am. I'm not going to play games with Ida Sue. I think maybe she's had enough games played with her in the past. I want her to know that, with me, what she sees is what she gets.

Ida Sue rolls over so that her upper body is over mine and she looks down at me. God she's so fucking beautiful, she makes me ache. Soft, honey brown hair, sparkling eyes and pouty lips made to give a man pleasure—along with a spark of sass to keep life interesting.

"You mean that don't you, Jan?" she asks, her voice filled with more than a little wonder.

I bring my hand up so I can play with the ends of her hair and I study her face. She's started calling me Jan. No one ever has before, and I don't think it would ever occur to me to let them. But, I like that Ida Sue calls me that. It's like she's claiming me as hers, taking a liberty no one else has ever had, one I've never given.

I'd give her anything.

"I mean it, Honey Girl," I tell her, giving her lips a brief kiss, as her body melts against mine.

"Where have you been all of my life?" she asks.

"Looking for you."

She may not know it, but that's the God's honest truth. She's the answer to every question, to every prayer, to every wish.

"If you don't stop being sweet, you're going to make me cry," she warns.

"I'll try to rein it in, Darlin'."

"I'd appreciate it," she says with a sweet smile that feels like it's all mine. *She feels like she's all mine.* "This has been the best Valentine's Day ever," she adds, kissing my chest.

"Shit," I mutter when I realize what she said. How I could have forgotten, I don't know, but I did. I need to remedy that really damn quick. "It's not over yet."

"It's not? You got another round left in you, Cowboy?"

"That's not what I meant, but with you I seem to always be ready," I tell her grabbing her hand and moving it down to hold it over my stiffening cock. Her soft hand wraps around my shaft and strokes me, but I stop her after that. There's something else that needs to happen first. "Hold that thought, Darlin'," I tell her, while stretching. I'm half on the bed and half off, stretching to pick up the jeans from where I dropped them earlier.

"What are you doing?" she laughs, but I'm turned to the side now, giving her my back so she can't see. "I wanna see!" She's giggling now, her hands on my back. She's happy and that makes me smile.

I sift through and find the pocket I stored the ring in earlier. It's just a simple diamond on a gold band, but I hope that Ida Sue can tell that it comes from the heart. I already have the matching gold wedding bands bought too. It might have been jumping the gun, but I know in my heart that she's the one. *Tonight just reinforced that for me.*

I open the box, letting my pants fall to the floor, and turn back on my back—ring hid in my fist.

"What are you doing, Cowboy?" Ida Sue grumbles, snuggling back into me and holding me close.

I open my hand to show her the ring.

"Ida Sue Lucas," I start, looking at her and then back to the ring. "Will you marry me?"

38

Ida Sue

OH GOD.

How can things go from good to horribly bad so quickly?

I look down at the ring that Jansen's holding and it feels like I have rocks in my stomach. It's beautiful, every woman's dream...

Except mine.

"Jan I..."

"I probably should have let you help pick the rings out, but I saw it in the window of the local jewelry store and it just seemed like you. Simple but beautiful," he adds and those rocks in my stomach seem to get heavier.

Shit...

"Ida Sue?" Jansen questions, when I don't reply. I tear my eyes away from the ring to look up at his face, and the confusion that I see there eats at me.

"Jan, honey, I..."

"Will you marry me?" he asks again.

"Jansen... I can't."

I feel his body go solid under me. It's as if there's a wall that's suddenly appeared between us. I hate it, I want to tear it down...*even as I'm the one nailing it up.*

"I see," he says quietly, his voice oddly calm. I get sick to my stomach, knowing this is going badly.

That's even more evident when the ring box slams shut and he moves, swinging his legs over the side of the mattress and sitting up. I'm left scrambling. When he goes to stand up, I practically tackle him, wrapping my arms around him and pressing my front to his back.

"No, Sweetheart, don't leave," I beg.

"I need to head back down to the barn. I apparently read everything the wrong way," he says, pulling against my hold. I refuse to let him go. I know in my heart that if I let him walk away, that will be it. It will be over and the thought of that happening makes me panic.

"I don't want you to go."

"There's no reason for me to stay, Ida Sue."

"There is. I'm here. Nothing's changed, Jansen. It hasn't. I—"

He pulls away from me, I try to hold him, but I can't. He stands and then turns to look down at me and that's when I see it. I can see the pain I've caused him, the hurt. I did that. The ironic thing is, I'm causing myself the same pain.

"Everything has changed, Ida Sue."

"No, it hasn't—"

"It has. The woman I love just turned down my marriage proposal. That's a *huge* change."

"It doesn't change the fact that I love you. It doesn't change what we are to each other."

"You love me?" Disbelief is thick in his voice.

"I love you so much Jansen."

"Then, why won't you marry me?"

His question destroys me. I don't know how to make him understand. I'm not even sure I understand myself.

"We haven't known each other that long, Jansen."

"It's long enough to know what I want, Ida Sue and what I want is right there in that bed."

"Believe it or not, Jansen, I know what I want, too and it's standing right there looking at me."

I think he listens to me, because his face softens—at least a little.

"Then, marry me, Lovey."

"I... I'm just not ready, Jansen. I'm not."

He rakes his hand through his rumpled hair and turns away from me. I hate that I'm doing this to him. I hate that I'm doing it to both of us. I'm a coward... *maybe*. I just... I can't say yes to him.

"What do you want from me, Ida Sue? I don't understand. I want us to belong to each other. I want you to be my wife."

"I can belong to you and not be married to you, Jansen. I already do belong to you. I love you. I don't need a piece of paper to prove that."

"Maybe I do, Lovey."

I can taste panic. My heartrate ramps up and my palms become sweaty. I don't want to lose Jansen.

"Can you just give me a little time?" I plead, praying I can at least stall him.

"Time?"

"I just need time, Jansen. Can you give that to me?"

I watch as he rubs the back of his neck, his gaze is appraising me. And I let him read me. I don't even try to put shields up. I need him to know I love him.

"I'm going to ask you again, Lovey."

"I know," I whisper. I don't want him too. I'm already dreading that phantom day in the future. Maybe if I show him how much I love him every day he will be happy enough. Maybe he won't demand marriage when he sees that I'm with him to stay.

That's a lot of maybes, but I have to have that hope. I don't want to lose Jansen.

It would destroy me.

"So, what now?" he asks and I can tell he's not happy, but he's pushing it aside for me.

I lick my lips nervously. "Make love to me, Jansen."

"Lovey—"

I don't want the fact that I don't want marriage to stand between us. I don't know how to make him understand. I don't even know how to explain myself to him. I just know I need to feel him inside of me. I need that closeness that happens when we're together.

"Please, Jan," I beg, letting the sheet I have pulled up against my chest drop down.

"You're mine, Ida Sue," he says.

"I am completely yours, Jansen," I vow as he walks toward me.

"I should be heading back to my place. Making love all night, when there are children in the house, is something married couples do," he says stubbornly.

"Committed couples do it, too, Jansen," I correct him.

"I don't feel right letting your kids know I'm up here with you and not as your husband."

"Haven't you heard that saying, Jan?" I ask, taking his hands in mine and pulling him down on the bed as I lie down, pulling him over my body.

"What saying?" he asks, his face buried into my neck as he begins kissing me there.

I angle my head to give him better access. Then, I reach down between us and take his cock in my hand. He's already hard and I revel in the fact that even though I hurt him, he still wants me. I don't know what I would have done if I destroyed this. I wasn't lying when I said I loved him. I don't know if I could survive without him...

And that's part of the problem.

I push that thought away as I stroke him.

"Lovey..."

"You feel so good, Jansen."

"If you don't stop that, this dance will be over before it even begins. What saying was I supposed to have heard," he growls near my ear.

"Why buy the cow when the milk is free," I whisper with a grin.

He pulls back to look at me. "Did you just call yourself a cow?"

I give him a mock mean look and stick my tongue out at him.

"I don't find the cow reference funny," he mutters.

"It's kind of funny," I retort. Then, I stroke him one more time and then position him at my entrance. I wrap my leg around him, letting the heel of my foot dig into his ass cheek, using it for leverage as I impale myself with his hard cock. "Yesssss…." I whisper in a long drawn out hiss of pleasure.

"You're a witch," he mutters, but he does it setting a rhythm as he slowly begins fucking me.

"I'm your witch," I remind him, just in case he forgets.

"Then, wear my ring," he says, proving he's one stubborn man.

"Shut up and fuck me, Jansen," I whimper as he thrusts deeply into me.

He grunts in reply, but his thrusts get harder and faster… I call that a win.

39

Jansen

"I'M as nervous as a cat on a hot tin roof, Jan," Ida Sue mutters, holding onto my hand like her life depended on it.

"There's no point, Lovey. Whatever happens, happens," I respond, trying to calm her. We're meeting with a lawyer two towns over. The Enrykers Oil Group contacted Ida Sue through him. I'm not sure what's going on—but, I do know that Ida Sue and I are hoping for two very different outcomes.

And that makes me a bastard.

If this turns out good for Ida Sue, it could be the answer to all her financial woes. It could erase so many problems for her. I want that for her, I do. It's just if this turns out that she gets money from this, she doesn't need me. She's already turned down my marriage proposal. If she becomes rich, she won't need me at all anymore.

Hell, maybe she never did.

"I know you're right, but think what this money could do for us," she mumbles, distractedly. My heart squeezes.

Us.

I know she's thinking about her and her kids, and that's what she should do. But, just for one fucking moment, I wish the us in her head… was me and her. I want to be that important to her. I want to be her partner.

I want to be her husband.

I know she said she wasn't ready. It wasn't a complete no. She said she loves me. It's just that when you ask the woman you love to share their life with you and they turn you down, it fucks with a man's head.

It's definitely fucking with mine.

"You and the kids will be good no matter what, Ida Sue. I'll take care of you."

I wonder if she can tell the anger and hurt in my voice. I try not to let it bleed through. I've never been the type of man who let things fester. I've always been straightforward. But, I've never experienced anything like this. I've never given a woman my heart and had a door shut with nothing but my foot trapped in it.

OR MAYBE MY DICK.

She seems to at least want that from me. In the two weeks since I gave her the table, we've been going at it like rabbits— at least whenever we can squeeze it in while the kids cooperate.

Meaning mostly while they are in school.

At night, I sneak up to her room through a damn tree like I'm a fucking teenager. I'm too old for that shit, and Ida Sue gives me hell about it. But, it's like I told her. I'm not about to let the kids think I've moved in. A man has his pride.

I'm from a throwback generation, I suppose. When the man was the head of the household and he took care of his woman and the kids. In my world that always came with a wedding certificate and a ring on your finger. I know people fuck up marriage more often than not. But, I'm not one of those people. Hell, as much as my ex-wife hurt me, I would have stayed married to her despite everything. When a man gives his vow, he sticks by it and he makes sure his woman never regrets saying yes.

That's who I am.

A dinosaur.

A dying breed.

And, there's probably a reason we're going extinct.

"Did you hear what I said, Cowboy?"

I look back down at her to see her smiling at me.

God, I love her.

Am I just an old fool?

"Sorry, Lovey. My mind wandered," I respond, my voice hoarse.

"I said, I know you will, but this money would make that easier. I don't like you working so hard all of the time."

I frown.

"A man ain't a man if he doesn't work, Lovey."

Her words annoy me. She should know that about me, right?

"I'm sorry Mr. and Mrs. Lucas. I was held up in a phone conference. I didn't mean to make you wait so long," the attorney says, coming back in the room.

"That's alright, Mr. Banks."

"We're not married. My name is Reed," I correct the lawyer when Ida Sue doesn't make a move to. "She's the only Lucas in here, besides the baby."

Ida Sue's face loses some of its color and the attorney looks a bit uncomfortable. And yeah, maybe it was me being a bastard, but I'm not about to let anyone call me a name that's not mine.

Especially now.

"I see. I apologize. If we could move into the office, there are some things I'd like to go over with you."

"I can take Mary and just sit out here, Lovey," I tell her, wanting to go in that room like I want to have my toenails removed.

Ida Sue stands up, while I'm still sitting. I reach up to take the baby and instead she puts her hand in mine.

"I want you with me, Jan. I need you with me," she says, her eyes pleading.

Well shit…

40

Ida Sue

I'M RICH.

Holy shit.

I'm rich!!!

It still hasn't sunk in. I sat in that small office while the lawyer talked numbers that seemed astronomical to me… and all I could think was….

I'm rich!

I was quiet the entire ride back into town. If Jansen wasn't with me, I'd have been in complete trouble, because I am sure I acted like a zombie. I've struggled my whole life. You don't have much choice when your parents kick you out before you're even out of school. I never dreamed anything like this would ever happen to me. Even now, two days later, I'm still having trouble thinking it's real.

"Lovey?"

My head jerks up to look at Jansen. It's late, or early— depending on how you look at it. I haven't checked but that damn internal alarm clock you seem to develop with children tells me it's close to four in the morning.

"Yeah?" I ask, giving him a squeeze. The room is mostly dark with the exception of a little moonlight from the window.

165

The house is blissfully quiet, and that rarely happens. I've been wrapped in Jansen's arms most of the night after making love with him and I can't remember a time in my life when I was ever happier.

Ever.

And it has nothing to do with the money. Although, I'd be lying if I didn't say that added to the happiness, because let's just be real.

I'm rich. I'm really stinking rich.

"Why do I feel like you're not here with me tonight?" he sighs and I immediately feel guilty.

"Sorry, Cowboy. I have this man who just gave it to me so good that I got zombie brain."

"Zombie brain?"

"Yep, where thought is not possible because your man just ate and ate ate…"

"I think you made that up," he laughs, but some of the tension leaves his body.

"You really know what you're doing between a woman's legs, Cowboy."

"Ida Sue—"

"Especially with your mouth. You should give lessons."

"Christ."

"Jansen's world famous—"

"World famous?"

"You're that good, Jan."

He shakes his head. "I guess it's good I have at least one use around here," he mutters under his breath.

"What are you talking about?"

"It's not like you need me around here, Ida Sue."

"Now, you're talking crazy. I love you, Jan. Even if you weren't needed at the ranch—which by the way, you totally are—I *need* you."

"Now that you have the money, Ida Sue, the last thing you need is a broken-down old cowboy."

"I think you just proved that you're not broken down," I respond, thinking he's being ridiculous. How he could even get the thought in his head that I don't want him is beyond me.

Jansen lets out a large annoyed breath and gets out of bed.

"Just what every man wants to hear."

"What are you talking about?"

"I'm talking about the fact I'm trying to have a serious conversation with you and instead you're more interested in my dick. I'm more than just what's between my legs, woman."

"Whoa. I was *joking* with you, dumbass."

"Nice. Real nice."

"What now?" I cry, exasperated.

"That just shows me how much respect you have for me," he growls, pulling up his jeans.

"What does?"

"Calling me a dumbass? That definitely shows me where I stand with you, Ida Sue."

"You are acting like a dumbass! If you rather I can call you a horse's ass. Better?"

"I'm leaving," he mutters, grabbing his shirt.

"You are not. We're going to talk about this, because that's what responsible couples do."

"What would you know about responsible couples?" he growls, sitting down on the bed, giving me his back and putting on his boots.

His words take my breath.

"That was low, Jan."

He finishes putting his boots on and he gets up, letting out another breath and this one sounds defeated. I should probably listen to the change in him, but right now, I'm hurt too.

"You're right, Lovey, it was," he says, leaning over to cup the side of my face in his strong hand. Mine immediately goes up to his, needing to hold onto him, needing something to fix whatever this is that has blown up between us.

"Jan, I do value you. I love you, honey."

"I love you, too. But it doesn't change things. Your life is changing and I'm not sure I have a place in it anymore."

"That's bullshit. You have a place, Jansen Reed. You have one right beside me. That's the only place I want you to be."

"And yet, you still won't marry me."

That ugly feeling from before coils in my stomach.

"You said you would give me time, Jan. You said you'd give me time," I whisper, terrified that I'm destroying the only man I've ever loved and not knowing how to keep from it…

41

Jansen

"FUCK. I know, Ida Sue. But damn it, can't you see this from my point of view?"

I rake my hand through my hair. I hate that I feel like I'm being unreasonable. It shouldn't be this hard when two people love each other.

Should it?

Fuck, I don't even know anymore. All I know is that I love this woman and every time I'm with her lately, it feels like she's slipping away from me. I'm a man that's used to being in control. The fact that I can't control the direction of this relationship is driving me insane.

"I can, but you're not listening to me."

"I am. That's the whole problem. I heard you tell me that you didn't want to marry me."

"*Right now.* I said right now, Jansen. I'm just not ready to marry anyone. I have a history, things you don't know about. Things we haven't discussed and those things have changed me. I don't want to get married and I don't see why that should be so important to you."

"You don't see why marrying you should be important to me…"

I say the words mostly to myself.

I repeat them.

I can't get how she can say that to me. I truly don't.

"I can't do this," I murmur, letting her face go and walking towards the door. Then, it hits me. I can't use the door.

I climbed up a fucking tree to get to my woman's room.

"Can't do what?" she says, and I can hear the panic in her voice.

"I can't argue with you right now. Not over this. Everything about you is important to me, Ida Sue. Every. Fucking. Thing. For you to lie in the bed we just made love in and tell me you don't see how you marrying me is important is like a damn slap in the face."

"But, I don't see. I love you! I've told you that I love you. How is a piece of paper going to change any of that?"

"It probably won't to anyone but me. I'm forty-four years old, Lovey. I want a home and a family."

"You have that, Jansen. This is your home. The kids and I love you. We're your family in every way that matters."

"Yeah," I say, shaking my head. There's no point in arguing with her that it's not in every way. She doesn't understand and maybe that's because at the core of the problem, she doesn't understand me.

Maybe she never will.

I seem to have a knack for picking women that I'm not enough for. I wasn't enough for my ex-wife because I couldn't have kids and now I'm not enough for Ida Sue to even consider tying herself to permanently.

I decided a while back that I'd just be alone the rest of my life. I should have remembered that decision instead of reaching for more.

"Jan—"

"Mommy, are you in there? I had a bad dream," Petal whispers through the door, her voice full of tears.

"Jan don't go. Let's talk about this," Ida Sue pleads.

"Ida Sue—"

"Mommy?" Petal asks again, turning the door knob that's locked. "Mommy, are you there?"

"Go tend to your baby, Ida Sue."

"Jan—"

"It's fine. We'll talk later," I tell her, lying through my teeth. It's not fine. I'm not sure it will ever be fine…. I walk over to the window and open it up.

"You could go out the door."

"You know my stance on that. Your kids don't need to see me come upstairs to fuck their mother."

She blinks at my words and I know they're harsh. I use the word fuck, but never in anger. Anger is dripping in my words now.

I get outside on the roof of the porch, dreading that damn tree, I close the window before Ida Sue can reply. She's got Petal to deal with and I need to clear my head. I manage to get onto the tree from the porch, even though my bones and joints protest. I'm holding onto the large limb when I notice a pair of eyes staring at me on the other side of the trunk.

"Gray."

"Jansen," Gray laughs.

"Why are you in a tree?" I mumble, knowing why I am, but Gray's a grown man.

"Moms are moms no matter what age you are," he says.

I nod, because I reckon that's true.

"Why are you in a tree?"

"Maybe it'd be better if we both never bring this up again," I compromise, not keen on hashing out why I refuse to let the kids know I spend my nights in Ida Sue's bed. They'd probably think I was as ancient as their mother is making me feel.

"I can agree with that."

"Good. Be careful getting back to your room."

"Had a lot of years of practice. You be careful jumping down from the bottom branch."

I grunt, and start moving down the tree again. Gray starts moving on up and as I take the small jump to the ground, my mood seems to have worsened instead of get better.

I've got to figure my shit out.

I'm just not sure what will happen once I do…

42

Ida Sue

I'M IN A PISS-POOR MOOD. I'll admit it, if only to myself. I've been working for that moron Mullins for way too long. They're to start drilling the oil on our land soon, but there's so much red tape I'm not sure when I will see the money. Which means I need to keep the jobs I have—at least for now, which unfortunately means I have to continue to work for Grave Mullins—and don't even get me started on that name. His momma must have known she'd want to kill him.

I only work for the idiot twice a week, but each day is getting harder and harder to stomach. His small put downs, the way he leers at me, and most of all the passes he keeps throwing my way that turn my stomach.

I'm so close to quitting, but then I remind myself of why I'm working. Until I see money in my hand from this oil, I can't trust it and there's a list a mile long of things that are demanding my attention.

The roof on the house will need to be replaced. Even now, I'm living in fear of the rain taking its toll. I can handle leaks, even if the buckets placed in strategic areas are annoying, but I know eventually the damage is going to become so substantial the rafters will begin to weaken.

I can barely afford our grocery bill now, so that's also a consideration. Then, there's the ratty, old, couch and chair that we're using now. I need to buy new furniture. There's just never been enough money for it all—even if purchased second hand. I figure groceries to feed everyone is more important than the table to put them on. I definitely could use another vehicle. Maggie taking me to work and dropping me off is getting old really fast.

Case in point, today.

Maggie is over thirty minutes late. I couldn't stand waiting on that asshole's porch any longer so I'm walking down the road and with Maggie's track record, I'll probably reach the house before Maggie remembers to come and get me.

And then there's Jansen.

I have no idea what I'm going to do with him. I swore off men. It would have been easier if I'd stuck to my guns on that one. But, I didn't. I fell in love with him and I know I'm losing him. I feel it. He's upset because I won't agree to marriage. I don't know how to make him understand my jumbled up thoughts, especially when I don't understand it myself.

He's not even come to my room the last couple of nights. He said he wasn't feeling well, but we both know there's this widening gulf between us. I don't know how to reach him and he won't get past this need he has for marriage. Why he even wants to saddle himself to a woman with nine kids is beyond me. Part of me wants to just say okay, I'll marry you, but the other part of me goes into a full-blown panic attack at the mere thought. Jansen doesn't understand me and if he thinks he's confused he should try living in my brain.

It's frustrating.

It's annoying.

It's… *baffling as hell.*

I'm thinking all of this over while staring at my feet, putting one foot in front of the other and being exhausted—emotionally as well as physically.

This person I am… it's not who I was supposed to be. It's not who I was meant to be. I don't know much, but I know that. There are some days I don't even like who I am. The only time I feel at peace is when Jansen is there, or was… that has changed since he began pressuring me for marriage. I need to fix us…

I just don't know how.

If it wasn't for my kids I would have given up long before now. They keep me going.

"Hop in."

I frown, looking up to see Jansen pulled to a stop in the middle of the road, beside me. I was lost in thought I guess, and didn't pay attention to passing vehicles. There's not been that many, hardly anyone travels these back roads anymore.

"I can—"

"Hop in, Ida Sue," Jansen replies, his voice stern. I instantly want to rebel, but really, I've been on my feet since five this morning and after cleaning three houses I'm exhausted. It's getting close to sundown and who's to know when Maggie will make her way out here. Tomorrow I'm taking the truck to work. I don't care if that leaves her stranded, it serves her right after the shit she's pulled today. I walk around the front of the truck and hop in.

"Thanks," I mumble, not sure how I feel about seeing Jansen or his abrupt order.

He could have at least said hello.

He puts the truck in drive, ignoring me. He doesn't say anything. He just keeps staring at the road ahead.

I stare out the passenger side window, too damn worn out to even begin to figure out what bee has crawled up his ass.

"I thought I told you not to walk the roads alone," Jansen growls about five minutes later.

I guess that answers what's wrong with him.

"Maggie forgot me, so I did what I had to do," I mumble, going back to looking out the window.

"What do you mean she forgot you?" he asks, like he's about to blow the top of his head off.

"Just what I said. She was supposed to pick me up over thirty minutes ago. She didn't show and I couldn't stand Grave Mullins any longer, so I left."

"What do you mean you couldn't stand him?"

"Why do you keep repeating everything I say?"

"Did that asshole say something to you?"

"I'm not getting into this with you," I tell him, giving my attention to the passing landscape once again.

"I asked a simple question, Ida Sue," he says and the fact he's trying to be logical pisses me off more than if he just barked another command at me.

This time I ignore him—*or my head might explode.*

"The least you could do is answer," he says, like he's a pouting child.

I don't need this. I have enough pouting kids in my life without adding a grown-ass man. A grown-ass man who honestly has been pissing me off for weeks now. I know he wants marriage, but damn it I told him I needed time. And what's wrong with just being with me without marriage? I'm a good woman. I told him I loved him. I told him I belonged to only him. What's he so pissy about? I'm worth waiting for my mind to clear up, damn it. So, I have a few miles on me, he has more! And yeah, I may have a lot of kids and maybe most men don't want to tackle that, but he knew I had those kids before he freaking slept with me!

"I'm not answering you, because now I've gone from being pissed at Grave Mullins to being pissed at you," I respond through gritted teeth.

"What are you pissed at me about?"

"You can't act like the jealous husband when you've been avoiding my bed for days, Cowboy."

"I can't act like the jealous husband anyway, because you won't marry me!"

"You said you'd give me time!"

"I've given you time, Ida Sue."

"The hell you have. You've done nothing but pressure me about it. I told you that I love you. Why isn't that enough, Jansen?"

"So, what do you want, Ida Sue? Do you expect us just to date for the rest of our lives, until you decide if I'm good enough for you?"

"That's not what I'm doing, you old coot. You're the best man I've ever known in my life. It has nothing to do with if you're good enough for me."

"Then what in the hell does it have to do with, Lovey, because I swear I'm lost on what comes next for us."

"Jansen, we haven't even known each other that long and you want me to jump into marriage."

"Are you so scared that your feelings for me will change?"

"No, Jansen," I respond and this time I barely whisper the words. I'm just too tired. "I just want to slow it down and take my time. I love you. That should be enough. Besides, we're not even really dating."

"That's funny, I could have sworn it's your lips I've been kissing practically every day, not to mention being in your bed."

"That's not what I meant. I meant, spending time getting to know each other."

"We see each other practically every day."

"I... Let me out."

"What?"

"Let me out of the truck."

"What for?"

"Because it's either get out of the truck or throw something at you and that would require more effort than you deserve," I growl.

"Woman—"

"Don't you woman me. I asked for time. I didn't turn you down. I didn't kick you out of my bed. I didn't say I didn't love you. *I just need time.* Either you're going to get that through your damn skull or you're not. At this point, I'm tired of fighting about it. You keep pressuring me, even if you say you aren't. What was it you told me, Jansen? That dating to you meant taking a girl out to dinner? We've never gone out on a date and here you are upset because I said no to marriage."

"I think we skipped the dating, Lovey."

"Yeah, I caught that. I'm not sure you have."

"You're right. I'm being a horse's ass," he sighs.

"I caught that, too," I grumble.

"You're going to hold a grudge, aren't you?"

"You haven't been in my bed for two days and you started a fight when I was already tired and had a headache."

"I take it that means yes."

I shrug, not bothering to deny it.

"If I come back to your bed tonight, will you forgive me?"

"That depends."

"On what?"

"Are you going to insist on climbing the tree like a fool?"

"Lovey—"

I reach in my pocket and pull out my housekey. "Come in after the kids are asleep if it makes you feel better. But stop risking your life by climbing in and out of a window like a damn teenager."

"I take it if I insist on coming through the window, you're not going to be happy," he mumbles.

"Let's just say if you show up in my window tonight, then you won't be petting the panty hamster and that'd be a damn shame."

"The panty hamster?" he laughs and I just shrug.

"I love you, Ida Sue," he says reaching out to pull me to him.

"I love you, too," I grumble, but I go and hold onto him tightly. I dodged a bullet this time.

I have to wonder how much longer I can.

43

Jansen

"JAN..."

She's whimpering my name. My cock buried so deep in her, she's clutching it so tight that I can barely breathe.

"Give it to me, Ida Sue. Give it to me," I growl, my hand holding her hip. I'm probably bruising her there, but if there's one thing I've learned about Ida Sue, it's that she likes it as rough as I do. She loves when I leave marks on her body, showing how carried away we both were. Hell, I like it too. I still have her bite marks on my shoulder from fucking her last night and I'm hoping she does it again before they fade.

"Harder, Jan..." she begs, her head tilting as she gasps out the words.

Her hands slap down on the table, holding onto the edge as I tunnel in and out of her—faster and harder than before. My gaze moves from her face, lost in pleasure, to the way her breasts move with each of my thrusts, bouncing with a rhythm that makes my hard cock swell even more.

"You're mine," I growl. "Completely mine."

The words are born from a need to have her submit, to have her admit that she needs me.

That she needs me as much as I need her.

She brings her leg up, opening herself up, causing me to sink impossibly deeper. So deep that I'm touching her womb.

"All yours." Her eyes open and she looks at me.

She's a sultress, a siren that has captured me. She reaches out and takes my free hand, bringing it to her sweet little cunt. Our fingers slide together over her throbbing clit.

"My sweet, little Honey Girl," I murmur, feeling my climax closing in.

I add pressure to her clit, moving our fingers over it in unison and then grinding down on it as my cock owns her body.

"Always yours, Jan. I love you." She struggles for breath, her eyes starting to close as her walls tremble around my shaft.

"Keep your eyes open, Ida Sue. I want to watch you come. I need to see you." Slowly her eyes open, just as she spasms around my cock. Her body jerks, and I feel her orgasm gush through her, bathing my cock as she writhes underneath me.

"That's it. That's my Honey Girl," I croon. Then, I let go, coming deep inside of her, painting her womb, and giving her another piece of me. She has most of them now. I can't keep from it. Love doesn't even begin to explain what I feel for her… What she is to me. I'm still hard even after I come. I seem to stay that way with Ida Sue. I pull her limp body up, still deep inside of her. Her legs lock around me and even though I just came, I feel my cock jerk inside of her, needing more. I carry her to the bar, which is a little higher and I place her on it, so I can look directly into her face. My hand brushes a stray tendril of hair, wet from the work out I just gave her body, from her face.

"What am I going to do with you, Ida Sue?"

"Keep me."

She smiles like it's just that simple. It's not. How can it be? Just this morning I found my paycheck on my desk. A paycheck signed by Ida Sue. I can't work for the woman I love. I already feel unsure of myself and that paycheck just cinched it. Things were different when the ranch was struggling. I was working to save it, to make it turn a profit for her. I had a purpose, a reason. Hell, after the money that was deposited into her accounts a couple of days ago… Ida Sue doesn't even need the ranch. In the past few days, I've gone from worrying about why she wouldn't marry me, to wondering why she should. I still don't have an answer.

"What's on your mind, Cowboy?" she asks, her face thoughtful as she brings her hand up to hold mine there against her face.

"I was just thinking that there's never been a more beautiful woman in the world."

It's kind of a lie, but it's not. It might not have been what I was thinking, but she's definitely the most beautiful woman I've ever seen in my life.

"There's no way that's true, but that's the one thing that always takes my breath when it comes to you, Jan."

"What's that?"

"The fact that you believe it. You never give me false compliments. You believe every word you give me."

"Always."

I bend down to kiss her lips, briefly. It's just a touch, but that's all that's needed.

"How long do you think we have before Mary wakes up and the kids are home from school?"

She looks over my shoulder at the old clock on the wall and then focuses back on me.

"I figure you have about thirty minutes, maybe forty if we're lucky."

"Then, I guess I better get busy," I grin.

"I guess so," she agrees, her hands pushing into my hair.

God… I love her. She loves me. It should be so simple.

Then why does it feel so hopeless?

44

Ida Sue

PEOPLE ARE LOWER than an egg sucking dog. Every day I believe that more and more. I've had money for a couple of weeks now and word has slowly spread through this little town. The change it has made in the way that people treat me has been shocking. I guess it shouldn't have been. I should have expected it, and in some ways maybe I did, but it has still been shocking.

I'm sure they still talk about me behind my back, but they're sweet as pie to my face.

Not that I give a rat's ass about any of it. I'm never going to be friends with these people. I have friends. I know who they are and they don't go talking shit behind my back—well maybe some do, but they say the same shit to my face and I can respect that.

Except for Julia—pronounced Jewel-ya in a long drawn out voice that makes you want to slap the shit out of her.

She still treats me like crap. Not that I expected much different. She was a bitch years ago when my parents threw me out. She's even more of a bitch now, if that's to be believed. She thinks her shit doesn't stink and that her life is perfect. How she could think that, since her husband keeps making passes at me on a daily basis, is beyond me. Maybe she doesn't care since she spends her time sleeping with Reverend Whitaker—and hiding that from Louise—Reverend Whitaker's wife.

Small towns... Got to love the deep dark secrets they pretend to hide.

Julia runs the only ladies clothing boutique in Mason. To be honest, most of my clothes and my children's clothes come from the Goodwill store a county over. I shop there often, mostly out of necessity, but also because kids grow so damn fast that it makes more sense to buy their clothes and not pay a fortune for them. Especially since my kids either ruin them playing or hit a growth spurt and outgrow them in a month. I'm actually planning on going there next week because Cyan and the twins are all outgrowing their britches—sadly, sometimes I think in several ways.

Those boys might be the death of me.

I take the dresses I just picked out for my girls, lay them over Mary's stroller handle and make my way to the front. Julia's sour face appraises me coolly. I avoid flipping her off and I feel like that's a win.

"Ida Sue. I didn't imagine seeing you in my shop."

"Now why is that Jules?" *(pronounced j'alls just to irritate the bitch.)*

Her nose scrunches up so much that I swear the woman looks like a damn English Boxer. *Of course, that might be an insult to the entire breed...*

"This just doesn't seem like *your* kind of shop," she says with a helpless shrug. "Although I did hear how you had come into money."

"And where would you have heard that?"

"Why, it's all over town. I guess it came at a good time too."

"Getting money doesn't usually have a bad time, Jules."

"It's Julia."

"Mmmm hmmm." I don't bother looking up and I'm not

going to change what I call her either. She should know that by now, but you can't fix stupid. "I'll take these dresses please."

I really shouldn't buy them, but I want my girls to have something pretty. I'll make it up to the boys by getting them that damn gaming system they've been begging me for. But, I want my girls to have clothes that make them feel beautiful. Every girl should have something that makes them feel beautiful. I didn't buy myself anything, but then there's nothing I want and if I ever need to feel beautiful all I have to do is look into Jansen's eyes.

God, I love that man.

"Word on the street is that you were losing your ranch, things were so bad," Julia murmurs, while taking the hangers off the dresses and folding them neatly on the checkout counter.

"Word would have been wrong." I smile sweetly at her. The smile is definitely forced, my lips are so stretched in sarcasm that it hurts and I'm grinding my teeth. I just want to throat punch her once.

Would that be so bad?

"That's not what I hear."

"Like I said, you heard wrong."

And she did. Things were definitely bad and I don't know how Jansen has done it, but he sent the bills out the last two months and there's a balance of twelve hundred dollars in the ranch account.

Now that my personal account is overflowing, I need to talk with Jansen on the best way to structure things. I want my kids taken care of and more money put in the ranch, to make it the kind of place it was always meant to be.

"Whatever you say, Ida Sue. You're probably right. It's best not everyone knows how bad things were."

"Jules, if you have something to say, just spit it out. I don't have all damn day to figure out what kind of snide insult you're trying to deliver."

Knocking Boots

"Obviously money can't buy good manners and decorum," she says shaking her head.

"Obviously, because you've had money your whole life and it hasn't helped you one damn bit," I snipe back.

"With your attitude it's a wonder you found a man like Jansen Reed who's willing to pay your bills," she responds. "That will be one hundred and eighty-two dollars. I'll throw in the change, unlike you I can rise above personal differences to help those less fortunate."

"What do you mean, Jansen pays my bills?" I narrow my eyes, bracing myself, because I'm pretty sure it's finally the right time to punch the cow.

"You didn't know," she smiles with glee.

"What are you talking about?"

"Jansen came in at the end of January and transferred money and caught the payments up on your place and paid three in advance."

"How do you know that?" I ask, but I know. Her husband works at the bank.

Mary picks that moment to start crying.

"Never mind," I snap at Julia, feeling like a fool a million times over. I throw two hundred dollars down on the counter, grab the bag of clothes and wheel Mary out of there. She needs a diaper change. The girl surely is dragging her feet learning to go potty. Most of my kids caught on quickly.

"You overpaid," Julia yells, right before the door closes. I catch it and turn to look at her. "If you think I'm one of those less fortunate you really haven't heard the amount of money I have now, Jules. Why I bet if I wanted to I could make sure your husband loses his fancy job at the bank for running his fool mouth."

I let the door slam on that threat. Then, I take a deep breath and try to figure out just what to do with the knowledge that Jansen used his money to save the ranch and lied to me about how we were turning a profit....

185

45

Jansen

I RUB the back of my neck and wonder for the millionth time if I'm doing the right thing or being a stubborn old fool. I still don't know the answer. I turn at the stop sign and head back into Mason. I've been three counties over today interviewing for a job as a foreman on a horse ranch. It's a good setup and the job is mine if I want it. I have to let them know by the end of the week.

I don't know if I can leave Ida Sue. I just know I can't stay on as her foreman when she doesn't even need me. I'm getting too old for the cattle business, horses are more my speed these days. I could do the cattle with some hired hands to help, sure. But if Ida Sue hires workers, then she *really* doesn't need me— not that I think she does anyway.

If I'm honest, I'm the one that needs her.

Life has gotten damn complicated.

I'm going to have to talk to her soon. I don't have a choice. At the last second, I decide to drive downtown. I need to transfer some more money from my personal account into the temporary one I opened up here in town. If Ida Sue thinks I'm going to cash the damn paychecks she keeps putting on my desk, she better think again.

I get into town and pull into the graveled parking lot across from the general store as if on autopilot. My head is too full of crap to pay much attention to anything, but as I'm walking toward the bank I see Ida Sue on the sidewalk. She's squatted down doing something with Mary. My heart hurts seeing her.

How am I supposed to leave her?

My feet automatically take me in her direction. She's like a magnet that I'm drawn to. She stands up, brushing her hair out of her face, so beautiful she makes me ache. There's never… *never*, been anyone in my life as beautiful as she is. It shines from the inside out.

I stop walking when I see Grave Mullins come up beside her to talk to her. He comes up behind her, catching Ida Sue off guard. He gets close to her—too fucking close. Then leans down to talk in her ear. Ida Sue smiles and I get this sick feeling in my stomach.

Jealousy fires through me like an asteroid intent on destruction. I've never been jealous in my life, but I'm definitely feeling it right now. I'm feeling it so much that I'm seeing fucking red. I take off running, intent on only one thing.

To tear Grave Mullins's head off his shoulders.

When I get there, Ida Sue is pushing him away. That should make me feel better, but I'm too far gone. I slam my hands into him. He stumbles, staggering and almost falling down, but not quite. Before he can get control however, my fist connects with his jaw. He takes a swing at me, I dodge it and punch him in the gut. He starts to go down but I push him against the side of the building as my fist connects again. After that, I truly lose it. I hit him over and over—stomach, ribs, face.

I take special joy in hitting the bastard in the face.

I probably would still be hitting him except Ida Sue swings her purse at me. It hits me on the side of the face and it's not a small purse. It's big enough to pack a damn basketball in. I don't know what she's got packed in it either, but the damn thing hurts more than being pistol whipped.

"Jan! Stop it! You're going to kill him."

"It'd be good enough for the son of a bitch."

"Maybe so, but he's not worth you going to prison."

"I'm not so sure."

"Fine then. Go ahead and be stupid and kill him," she growls.

I didn't really need her permission, but since I have it, I kick the bastard in the crotch.

Ida Sue swings her purse of death at me again.

"Damn it, Lovey! That hurts."

"Good! I swear Jansen Reed, if you get arrested and thrown in jail I'm not bringing you any soap on a rope."

"What?"

"You heard me mister. You will just have to use the prison issued stuff and if you drop it, that's not my problem."

"Lovey—"

"If you want to be Cell Block A's prime real estate for a game of butt darts, that's your business, Jan," she grumbles, then she turns around and pushes Mary's stroller farther down the sidewalk.

"Stay away from Ida Sue or I'll finish what I started," I threaten Mullins.

"I'm going to sue you!"

"Try it and I'll make you sorry you were born," I warn him, and I'm not even kidding. Then I turn and chase down Ida Sue, who is almost at the parking lot by now. "Damn it, Ida Sue!"

"Don't talk to me. I can't believe you right now."

"He had his hands on you!"

"So?!?! I was handling it."

"Yeah, I saw just how you were handling it."

"What in damnation are you going on about now?" she mutters, opening her truck door and carefully taking Mary out of her stroller.

"Bites…" Mary demands.

"Okay, baby. Let's get you in the car seat and we'll find you some food," she promises.

I take Mary out of her hands and put her in her seat. Mary goes from whining and not wanting in the seat to grabbing my hat and pulling it off my head. I get her buckled in and manage to trade my hat to Mary by handing her one of her toys that's in the seat. I close the door and walk to Ida Sue's door. She's closed in her truck now, but the window is down.

"What did you mean you saw how I was handling it?" she asks again, her eyes narrowed and her forehead wrinkled with anger.

"You were smiling at him and rubbed your backside against him. Don't bothering denying it, Ida Sue. I saw you," I accuse her, my hat still in my hands.

I thought I had seen Ida Sue angry before. I really had. Right now, I know that I haven't. I've only seen her aggravated, because right now I can see that she is *furious*.

"You're a horse's ass. I thought he was you, you jerk!"

"Not likely! We don't look anything alike!"

"My back was turned to him! You're the only man I'd expect to get near me like that! I seriously can't believe you right now!"

"Ida Sue—"

"I'm taking Mary to get her some food and you better pray I've calmed down by the time I get back home."

"Maybe you better hope I've calmed down!"

"Why, Jan? I'm not the one that's been lying this whole time."

"Woman, I've never lied to you!"

"Really, Jan? Then how come I was just told by the one woman in this whole county that I'd have trouble spitting on if she was on fire—and let me tell you Jansen, I'd love to spit on her any other time—"

"Ida—"

"I had to hear from her that you were the one that paid the

ranch payments, and not by the so-called profit we've been making!"

Fuck.

"Darlin'…"

"Go darlin' someone else, Cowboy. You *knew* how important it was to me to know what was going on with the ranch. You *knew* I needed you to be upfront and honest with me. Instead, I find out you've been doing shit you had no right to do behind my back!"

"If I hadn't you were going to lose the ranch!"

"Then I'd have lost the ranch! It was my ranch to lose! Not yours, Jan! I've been through worse; my kids have been through worse. We would have survived."

"And that right there is the whole problem," I tell her. My mind finally made. I guess if you want to get technical, Ida Sue made it up for me.

"What are you talking about now?"

"It was *your* ranch to lose. I don't have a right to try and save it for you and the kids. No wonder you won't marry me, Ida Sue. You only think in terms of you and your kids. You don't have room for me in your life."

"Jan—"

"I'll be leaving at the end of the week. You have money now. You can hire someone to take my place, or not… like you just made abundantly clear, it's not my problem."

I walk away after that, putting my hat on and going to my truck.

It's over.

46

Ida Sue

"WELL, Ida Sue... you've certainly stepped in it now," I mutter to myself.

I'm leaning over the kitchen sink, watching Jansen load up his truck. He doesn't have a lot, but he's leaving in the morning and watching him throw his saddle and things in the back of his truck hurts more than I could ever put into words. I've tried to talk to him. I got nowhere. It didn't help that I had no idea what to say to him. He's right. I shouldn't have made him feel like he didn't have a say when it came to the ranch and what happens in my life and that of my kids. I didn't mean it like that, not really. It was just words spit out in the heat of anger, but I don't know how to make it better. I don't have a clue.

"Is Jansen really leaving tomorrow?" Maggie asks from behind me.

"I'm afraid so."

"But, you love him."

"Sometimes love isn't enough," I murmur, ignoring the sting of tears that brings.

"But he loves you too. He told us he did," Cyan yells.

I turn away from the window to see all of my kids standing there looking at me. Several are looking at me with sadness.

Petal and Cyan's faces look more like panic—an emotion I can completely identify with right now. Green is looking at me with anger though.

"He does. Being an adult is complicated sometimes—" I start and that sounds lame even to my own ears.

"You need to fix this, Mom," Gray says from the door. He and White are standing there and I frown.

"Why aren't you two in school?" I ask, knowing good and well they should be there, it's the middle of the week.

"Green called and told us that Jansen was planning on leaving. We came to stop that."

"Good luck, he's dead set on leaving," I mutter.

"Only because you're being stubborn."

I look at White. Of all my children, White and Gray have been the ones I've relied on the most… probably because we grew up together. Sometimes I think they are more adult than me.

"I can't—"

"I don't want to lose Jansen! I love him!" Petal says, stomping her foot and running off to cry.

I let out a long, sad sigh.

This is a damn mess.

"Mom—"

"I can't hear anymore tonight," I tell Black. "Relationships are complicated and there's a lot you don't know about, son. I'm not about to get lectured by my fourteen-year-old son. I'm going to go see to your sister. Since you're all standing around with nothing to do, you can clean the kitchen up tonight," I mutter and then I head upstairs to see if I can console my daughter's broken heart.

I just wish someone would do the same with mine…

```
┌─────────────────────────────┐
│                             │
│            47               │
│                             │
│           Gray              │
│                             │
└─────────────────────────────┘
```

"DAMN THIS IS A NICE SET UP," I mutter looking around the playhouse.

"We worked our asses off on it," Black mutters.

"Get real, you bailed out after a couple of hours and went fishing with your buddies," Blue tells him.

"Whatever. I worked twice as hard as you did all week in those two hours."

Black flips Blue off and I laugh. Those two are just like me and White when we're together.

"You're both crazy. We all know Jansen did most of the work," Green grumbles.

"Yeah," Maggie says with a sigh, sitting at the table in the back. She's dejected and that's unlike Maggie. She's usually in charge when it comes to group meetings with the siblings.

"Mags? You okay?"

"No. I'm not okay."

"What about you Petal?" I ask, because there's not much I can say to Maggie. None of us are okay that Jansen is going to leave. Even White and I are upset and we aren't here most of the time. Still, we both know that this is the first time Mom has been this happy. Plus, damn it, she needs someone to take care of her. White and I are coming back from school as much as possible, but it's causing problems with work and school. The two of us are staying exhausted lately, trying to balance everything. College is supposed to be the best time of your life. So far, it's been nothing but work.

"Mom gave me ice cream," she says through sniffles—which I guess is five-year-old speak for she's okay.

"So what are we going to do?" I ask my brothers and sisters. For as long as I can remember, we've always gotten together like this and worked things out when shit got bad. Mom taught us that. Family first, and we all work together to make the changes we need. Usually she's with us, it just so happens this time she's part of the shit that needs worked out. I love my Mom. She's the strongest person I know, but right now she needs to get out of her own head. She can't lose Jansen.

None of us want to lose Jansen.

"There's nothing we can do. Except maybe eat ice cream like Petal," Maggie says dejectedly.

"Bullshit on that. I say we march in and tell mom to get her head out of her ass and fix this mess."

I look back over at Cyan and laugh.

"Baby brother if you tell Mom to get her head out of her ass there won't be enough of us to find all the pieces of you strung over Texas," White laughs.

"She wouldn't hurt me," Cyan argues stubbornly.

"She might not, but she'd put the hurt *on* you," Maggie says.

"That's for damn sure," Green laughs.

"Okay fine then, what are we going to do?"

I look at Cyan, wishing I had the answer.

"I don't understand any of this. Mom loves Jansen," Maggie mutters.

"Yeah and it's clear that Jansen loves her. He even asked her to marry him," I agree, frowning, wondering how we got from that to Jansen leaving now.

"I didn't think we needed him from the beginning," Blue says and all of us look at him, ready to fight.

"That's because you're—"

"But, he beat up Grave Mullins in town. So, I think that makes him good in my book," Blue adds, interrupting his twin.

"Shit. He beat that asshole up?" White asks, clearly impressed.

"Yeah, dude. That's all anyone was talking about when I was there. Grave couldn't even walk when Jansen was done with him. Sam and Walter from the garage had to help him up."

"Damn, wish I could have seen that," I mumble.

"You not supposed to say damn, Gray," Petal says, vanilla ice cream dripping from her chin.

"What about White? He said shit," I remind her.

"That's okay. White won't get in trouble."

"Why won't White get in trouble?"

"Cause he's oldest."

Petal's reply is hard to make out, because she's got her tongue stretched out to the right of her face and trying to lick the ice cream. My sister is a mess, but damn she's cute.

"That's right. I'm oldest."

"Fine, old man, what do we do to fix this mess?"

"We have to get them together," he says like it's the simplest thing in the world.

"How are we going to do that?"

"We were going to do it before, they just worked things out first. So, we do it now. We lock them up somewhere together and let them fight it out."

"Mom will kill him if he pisses her off," Green warns.

"Jansen can hold his own," Black argues.

"Fine. Where can we lock them up together? The house has too many exits."

"That wouldn't work anyway numb-skull," Black tells Cyan. "You can't lock someone in the house, the locks are on the inside."

195

"Whatever. How about the old outhouse down by the pond?"

"*The outhouse?*" Maggie screeches.

"Yeah! It's got a lock on the outside. Remember when Blue locked Black in there? Hah, I thought he was going to kill Blue when he got out!"

Cyan's laughing as he remembers. It was pretty funny. It happened a few years ago and Black doesn't like the dark so he kind of panicked.

"I didn't think that was funny," Black pouts.

"You wouldn't. You were too busy screeching like a little girl," Blue laughs.

"Asshole," Black mutters flipping Blue off again. "Besides I got out pretty quick."

"You do have a gift for breaking and entering," White agrees.

"It's a gift." Black leans back in one of the wooden chairs that Jansen put in here and smiles like he owns the world.

"Yeah, it will probably come in handy when they throw him in jail. Maybe you can get out of the jail cell when they arrest you for breaking into Niecy Jane's house," Green says.

"The law won't have to arrest him if Niecy's dad catches him," White responds and that's the damn truth. I need to have a talk with my brother before he gets himself killed. This is stuff Jansen could handle if he was here. Then, I wouldn't feel so guilty for being away all the time. I love my siblings, but damn they're exhausting sometimes.

"Mom and Jansen aren't going to talk things out in an outhouse. You don't make up from a fight in a small box that smells like…" Maggie trails off looking at Petal.

"Shit," White adds with a wink. Maggie rolls her eyes.

"Maybe we could have them arrested and they could talk things out while they're in jail?"

"That's a great idea moron."

"Hey, I thought so. There's handcuffs at the police station. Jansen could use them on Mom," Black tells Blue.

"The dummy has a point there," Maggie says. "You'd have to handcuff Mom to get her to listen."

"That's not what I was thinking you could do with the handcuffs, but whatever." Black grins.

"It's a wonder I haven't killed my brothers before now," Maggie says, while sighing dramatically.

"I don't want Mommy in jail!" Petal cries. "If she goes to jail they'll take us away from her. It happened to my friend Alice!"

She starts crying and Cyan picks her up and puts her in his lap. He's only six years older than Petal, but he's tall like the rest of us boys and looks a lot older. Which could be really bad, because he's growing up much faster than he should. Hell, even I notice that. Mom is constantly worrying about him.

"I didn't know that happened to Alice," Cyan says, petting Petal's hair.

"Yeah. She's living with her aunt now. I don't want to live with my aunt, Cyan. Alice says her aunt is mean. I don't even know my aunt, but I bet she's mean, too."

"Mom's not getting arrested, Pet. It's okay," Cyan calms her.

"Yeah, Pet, we're just kidding," Black adds, feeling guilty and he comes and takes Petal out of Cyan's arms.

"What about this playhouse? It's big in here," I suggest.

"There's no lock," White points out.

"We could wedge the door closed with one of those old, fence posts that Jansen replaced down by the barn."

I think about Blue's suggestion, but I shake my head no.

"Jansen would just knock it loose. If he really took down Grave Mullins like you said, he packs a punch."

"True," he agrees.

"It wouldn't do any good," White adds. "There's a window. Mom would bust it open and escape."

"Or Jansen would. You know how Mom gets when she's mad," I answer with a nod. "So, this place is out."

"What about the tack room? It's nice."

"It stinks like horse feed and saddles in there," Maggie complains while curling her nose.

"True, but there is that couch in there so they could... *sit* and talk," White says with a wink in my direction.

I ignore the icky images that come to mind with his wink.

"It locks from the outside, too," Green adds.

"The door is definitely solid. Jansen wouldn't be able to break it open," Black agrees.

"And there aren't any windows," Blue says, while nodding.

"That's it then. We lock them up in the tack room," I announce, feeling better now that we've concluded things and come down with a plan.

"That just leaves one problem," Blue responds while everyone is congratulating each other on the plan. We all stop to look at him. "How are we going to lure them both to the tack room when they won't even look at each other? Not to mention Jansen will be leaving in the morning."

"We need something to lure them both there," I respond, a plan already forming in my head.

"What would lure them both there together, when they can't stand to even look at each other now?" Maggie asks.

"We use the one person we all have a weakness for in this family," I laugh, thinking it might just be that simple.

"Who's that?"

All of my brothers and sisters look at me, each asking that question at the same time and looking at me like I'm crazy.

All except one.

"Me!" Petal exclaims, proving she's smarter than any normal five-year-old. But, then again, she is a Lucas...

48

Jansen

I CAN'T PUT it off any longer. I've been dragging my feet because I don't want to leave. I thought Ida Sue would cave. I thought she would at least try to stop me. She hasn't even come down here. She just keeps standing on the porch watching me.

I'm holding the key to the office and to the quarters I've been staying in. I suppose I'll have to be the one to walk them up to her. The least she could do is come down and get those. It sticks in a man's craw to have the woman he loves not even bothering to come say goodbye.

I'm about to bite the bullet when Gray and White come up.

"Didn't know you two were home."

I clear my throat to talk, when it becomes obvious they aren't going to. They're just standing there looking at me.

"We came home to keep an eye on mom when we heard you were leaving," Gray says, watching me closely.

"That's good. She needs that."

"She needs a man who won't give up," White responds, his voice solid. I eye them both up and down. They're old enough to get it, and if they want me to lay it out for them, I'll lay it out.

"I tried to be that man. Ida Sue wouldn't let me."

"Didn't figure you for the kind of man who would quit, Jansen."

My head jerks at that and it comes from Blue as he and Black show up behind their brothers. Of all of Ida Sue's kids, Blue's been the one that's been the most distant. He's gotten a little more relaxed around me, but I know that he's been the one that's the most standoffish for sure.

"If she gave me any indication that she wanted me to stay, maybe I wouldn't."

"She's been crying all night and she's standing up there watching you now with tears in her eyes, that doesn't count?" Black asks.

I frown. It should count and maybe it would, but other things matter, too. Like the fact that I can't make my living off the woman I'm sleeping with. If we aren't married then I'm just a kept man and that eats at me. Hell, it might even with the damn ring, but at least I'd feel a little better about it all.

"What's going on is between your momma and me, boys. Maybe it's better if we just leave it at that."

"I don't want you to go, Jansen," Petal cries, running in between her brothers and tackling me by wrapping her arms around my legs.

There's nothing on this earth that cuts your heart out faster than the sound of a little girl crying for you.

I bend down and pick Petal up in my arms and bring her to me.

"Don't cry, Muffin. I don't like to see your tears."

"I want you to stay and be my Daddy," she whimpers, burying her head in my neck. I feel her tears drip against my neck and I hold her tightly as her body shakes with her sobs.

"I don't want to go either," I admit.

"Then stay!" she pleads, looking back at me.

"It's not always that simple, Sweetheart."

"It is if you love us, Jansen. Don't you love us?" she asks.

"I do love you. More than you will ever know."

"Don't you love my brothers and sisters?"

"I love all of you," I tell them, looking at each one of them, needing them to know I do care about each of them.

"Then, stay," Petal begs, hugging me tight again.

"Being an adult is complicated, Petal. Sometimes you don't get what you want the most."

"I don't want to lose you, Jansen."

"You don't have to. I'll let you guys know where I end up. You can write me and keep in touch."

"But, Jansen. I'm only five. I don't know how to write."

"Maggie can help you, or you can call me. You know your numbers, right?"

"Yeah…"

"Then you can call me. I'll always be here for you Petal." I look up at the other children standing around me and Maggie has joined us now, too. "I'll always be here for any of you. You just have to reach out. Whatever you need, I'll be there for you."

"So, you won't just dis'speer?" Petal asks and I smile despite the sadness that I'm choking on.

"I won't. In fact, one day I'm going to be back to watch you get married."

"Ew. Boys are icky."

"You keep thinking that, Muffin. Now, give me a hug. Old Jansen's got to get moving."

She hugs me, and once I help her down she takes Maggie's hands.

"Just for the record, I don't want you to go either, Jansen."

"Just for the record—again—I don't want to go," I tell her with a sad smile.

"You better not just disappear. And I do like boys, Jansen. And one day I'm going to get married and I'm going to want you to walk me down the aisle."

I swallow down the wave of emotion that causes.

"I'd be honored Maggie."

"Let's go look at the new colt, Petal," Maggie says, taking

Petal away. She's probably trying to distract her and I have to admit, I'm grateful for that.

"Is it time?" Petal asks. I blink at the strange question. Maybe she's asking if it's time for me to leave. It is… it's past time.

"Yeah, it's time," Maggie murmurs, echoing my own thoughts. I watch as the girls walk away and then the boys all come up and shake my hand. Each goodbye makes this harder and harder. It's like going through hell one goodbye at a time.

Finally, Cyan walks to me. He's tall, looking more like the twins age than eleven. I hold out my hand to him and he looks at it. Then, he surprises the hell out of me.

He hugs me. I wrap my arms around him and I swear to God it hurts to breathe now.

"Love you, Jansen."

His voice is barely more than a whisper, but his words pierce inside of me and they make a wound that I know will never heal. I don't know how I became so entrenched in this family so quickly, but what I do know is that they were meant to be mine.

I just don't know how to make Ida Sue realize that…

I FEEL like I'm dying inside.

There's no other way to put it.

I should be used to men leaving. I should be used to being on my own. It should be a familiar place to be and it shouldn't hurt this damn much. The thing is, however, that with Jansen it hurts more. It hurts even more than it did when my own father turned his back on me. It's all I can do right now to remain standing. If I weren't leaning on the front porch post, then my knees most assuredly wouldn't hold me up.

"Ida Sue," he says as he gets to the bottom of the steps.

"You're ready to leave?" I ask him, my heart feeling like it's being squeezed in a tight fist.

"Do I have any reason to stay?" he asks and if I didn't love him so much, I'd hate the man right now.

"I've told you that I love you and it's clear my kids love you. If that's not enough to make you stay Jan, then I don't really know what you're looking for here."

Say you'll stay. Say I'm worth staying for.

Inside I'm pleading for him to say that. I'm begging him to choose me and not walk away. I can't tell him that, though.

I can't.

"I don't want to rehash this, Ida Sue," he says instead and I guess that's about as far away from what I want him to say as you can get.

"Then don't," I respond simply, even though I feel like I'm dying.

His face goes hard and he nods once.

"Here's your keys. You'll need them for whoever you hire to take my place," he says reaching out to hand them to me.

Three small gold keys. They shouldn't bother me. One to the tack room, one to the ranch hand quarters…. But, that third one… that third one nearly destroys me. It's the key to the house. The house he wouldn't stay in, the house he didn't want the kids to know he slept in.

I swallow down the bitterness. There's no point in letting it out, not in front of Jansen. Later, after he's gone and the kids are in bed and I can let it out, then I'll cry. Then, I'll let myself bleed.

I reach to take them. My hand feels ice cold, my fingers frozen. They graze against his rough, warm hands and I close my eyes trying to memorize them. It's a moment of weakness, and I know he can see the pain on my face, because his hand suddenly wraps around mine. I open my eyes to look at him, knowing there are tears showing, waiting to be shed.

"Lovey…"

"It's okay, Jan. I understand," I tell him, and I do.

I'm not enough.

I've never been enough, not for anyone.

"I wish to hell someone would explain it to me," he growls. He grabs the hat off his head and pushes his hand through his hair, a move I've started recognizing that shows frustration. "Because I have to tell you, Lovey, I don't understand any of it."

"Then why are you—"

"Mom! Jansen! Hurry! Come to the barn!" Maggie cries, her voice sounding panicked.

"What's wrong?" I yell out, fear instantly filling me. Something is wrong, horribly wrong—I can tell it in Magnolia's voice.

"It's Petal. She's in the tack room. Something's wrong. She fell and I can't get her up!"

Jansen takes off running and I follow him, my heart in my throat.

Please God, don't let anything be wrong with my baby.

Please....

"WHERE IS SHE?" I cry, and I'm side by side with Jansen by the time we hit the barn.

"She's in the tack room behind the couch," Maggie responds.

I run to the tack room and step in, heading to the back of the room where the couch is.

"Maggie go back to the house and call 911," Jansen says from behind me.

God, I didn't even think to call for an ambulance. Thank God Jansen is more together than I am.

"Jan…"

"She'll be okay, Lovey," he says, his hand at my back as we round the couch and go behind it.

"Maggie, she's not here. Maybe she…"

"Hi, Mommy."

My head jerks up when I hear Petal's voice. I straighten up and stand beside Jansen confused.

"Petal, baby. Are you okay?"

"Yep! I'm fine. Don't be mad, Mommy."

"Don't be mad? Petal let's get you to the doctor."

I start walking toward her and she steps back and shuts the door.

"What in the hell?" Jansen growls.

We walk faster toward the door. I don't know what the kids are up to, but something is definitely going on. I make it to the door and I try to open it, but the door is locked.

"It's locked."

"It sticks sometimes," Jansen says and I move back so he can open it.

"It's locked," he says when he can't open it either.

"Isn't that what I just said?" I mutter.

"Mom?"

"White? Open the door. Petal accidentally locked it. Tell Maggie to cancel the ambulance and—"

"Mom, don't be mad," White repeats Petal's words.

"Mad? What in the hell is going on here?" I ask, the worry over Petal starting to leave and the realization that my kids are definitely up to something, taking its place.

"You and Jansen needed to talk things out," Maggie says from the other side of the door.

"We've already talked about things," I argue.

"But you didn't work things out, because Jansen is leaving," Gray adds.

"Jesus," Jansen mutters under his breath.

"We don't want Jansen to leave, Mom."

This time it's Cyan talking.

"We want him to stay," Black joins in, giving his two-cents.

"You love him, Mom and he loves you."

I hold my head down as I hear Green.

"I told you kids, sometimes love is not enough," I remind them.

"We're not letting Jansen leave," Petal yells.

"Yeah, we're keeping him," Cyan chimes in.

"Boys, that's not the way this works," I tell them with a tired sigh.

"You need to talk it out, Mom. Just because life gets hard, it doesn't mean you give up. You taught us that, remember?"

I hate it when Maggie uses my words against me. She's been doing it more and more lately.

"Jansen?"

"Yeah, Blue?"

"We all want you to stay."

"Son…"

"We're keeping you Jansen," Petal sing-songs.

"We'll be back later," White says and I hear them moving around outside.

"You kids open this door right now, or so help me when I get out of here I'll make your rear-ends so red that people will think Rudolph is bending over and smelling Santa's ass!" I yell.

"That doesn't make sense, Mom."

"It doesn't have to make sense, White. Open this damn door!"

"We'll come let you out in the morning. There's sandwiches and cola in the fridge," he says instead.

"White, damn it!" I yell banging on the door.

Silence.

"I'm warning you kids, you better open this door right now!"

"I don't think they're out there, Ida Sue."

"I'm going to kill them," I mutter.

"No, you won't," he says.

"What are we going to do?"

"Wait until your kids come and let us out."

"We can't stay in here all night, Jansen."

"I don't think we have a choice."

I look around the room, frowning.

"We can't stay here," I mutter again, trying to find something to knock the door down.

"You said that already. What's wrong, Lovey? Scared?"

My head jerks up to look at him. I try to swallow my panic

down, but it doesn't really work. He's wrong I'm not merely scared.

I'm petrified....

51

Jansen

"BUST THE DOOR DOWN."

I turn to look at Ida Sue, unable to hide the shock on my face.

"You want me to bust the door down?"

"That's what I just said."

"Ida Sue, I'm not going to bust the door down."

"Why not?"

She actually whines the words like a two-year-old would when she doesn't get her way.

"Ida Sue, that door is solid."

"So?"

"It's not like we're in danger. The kids will be back to let us out."

"I'm not staying in here overnight. I have things to do. I have to work!"

"Yeah, right," I answer, suddenly just tired of it all. Then, I walk back to the couch, plopping down on it and wishing there was a television. I don't watch much of it, but right now it might be a good distraction.

"What's that supposed to mean?" Ida Sue huffs.

She follows me, standing in front of the couch as I stretch

out on it. I kick off my boots, letting them fall haphazardly to the floor, pull my hat down so it covers my face, and settle in.

"Of the two of us here, Ida Sue, I'm the one that needs to get to work. The last thing you need to do is work."

"Are you taking a nap right now?" she cries.

"I am if you'd stop your caterwauling."

"Caterwauling? Did you just say that to me? Do you not realize that we're locked in this damn room alone until my kids decide to come let us out?"

"Gee, I guess that might have slipped my mind."

"Now is not the time to be sarcastic, Jansen. We need to get out of here."

"Then, quit giving me the opportunity."

"Fine, if you aren't going to help me out of here, I'll find a way myself," she announces.

"Sounds good.

I close my eyes, knowing there's not a chance I'm going to go to sleep, but at least with the hat over my face and my eyes shut I might be able to ignore the fact that I'm in here with Ida Sue. If I'm honest, I have too much shit swirling in my head. I didn't expect the kids to pull this. I didn't expect them to… *claim* me. What does a man do when nine kids lay claim to him and do everything they can to stop him from leaving?

If only their mother showed that kind of emotion…

I'm so lost in my thoughts, that I jerk when a large noise echoes through the room. I frown, wondering if I dreamed it and then it happens again. I yank the hat off my face and turn to look around the room and there's Ida Sue.

She has an old metal horse comb and is beating against the door with it.

"What in the tarnation are you doing?" I ask, still not quite believing my eyes.

"I'm trying to get out of here," she says, beating on the door.

"What are you going to do, brush the door down?" I laugh.

"I'm trying to loosen the knob wise guy. If you'd help me, it might actually work!"

"In no universe is a metal curry comb going to get us out of here, Ida Sue."

"Fine then," she growls.

She's not finished, however. She throws the comb at me, it swings wide and misses me by a mile, but I get up off the couch, stomping towards her—*pissed.*

"What in the hell is that for?"

"You need to help me get out of here!"

"What's the big damn deal? The kids will get tired and let us out eventually."

"I have to get to work!"

She screams the words, but that's not what bothers me. There are tears in her eyes and that's what has me by the damn balls.

"Are you crying because you're not going to work? Jesus Christ, woman! You're rich. You don't need to work, you don't need anything or anyone!"

"If that's what you think, then you never really knew me at all, Jansen Reed."

"That's what I know! Have you noticed the amount of money in your bank account? You don't need to fucking work and scrub toilets for assholes like Grave Mullins anymore, Ida Sue."

"I do!"

"You don't!"

"I do!" she repeats, stubbornly.

"Why?"

"Because it won't last!"

I blink.

"What are you talking about now?"

"It won't last, Jansen. Nothing good ever lasts and the more I try to make it last… the more it hurts when it leaves."

"Darlin', you could retire and live happily on what's in your account now. It won't disappear, it's already there."

"I couldn't," she says, and I shake my head. "You could especially when you factor in the payments you haven't received yet that are coming—"

"I can't live happily, Jan. I'll never have that."

"Ida Sue—"

"You're leaving. Without you, I'll never be happy," she finally says, tears falling from her eyes.

Christ.

52

Ida Sue

IT'S TOO MUCH. All of it is just too much. Watching Jansen pack, watching my kids say goodbye to him, thinking Petal was hurt, having the kids pull this stunt and finally being alone in a room with Jansen—knowing he's leaving and having him treat me like a stranger.

It's all just too much.

I didn't plan on breaking down. I didn't want him to see that, but there's no way I can keep from it. I'm too overloaded with it all.

"Ida Sue, what am I supposed to say to that?"

"Nothing. It's not your problem," I tell him, avoiding looking at him and feeling like a fool a million times over.

"It fucking is my problem. I offered to marry you woman. If that's not a sign I was planning on staying I don't know what the hell is!"

I've never reacted well to people screaming at me. I admit that freely. Right now, however, I want to hate Jansen. I want to hate him for hurting me, for hurting my kids, for leaving… for making me believe in love again… for so many things I can't keep them all straight. So, I snap.

"And yet, here you are, Jansen! *Still leaving!*"

"Woman, don't hand me that shit!"

"I'm just telling the truth! If that's too hot for you to handle, get out of the kitchen!"

"We're not in the kitchen!"

"Stop screaming at me!"

He growls like a bear, turning his back to me. I start moving through the room to see if I can find anything to pry the door open with. If it wasn't locked with a damn deadbolt I'd be home free.

"Ida Sue, you're the one that turned me down. If you wanted me to stay, all you had to do was say you'd marry me," he says and his voice is calmer now, weary.

He can join the crowd, I'm feeling the exact same way. I look up from the corner that I'm in, going through the horse grooming tray to stare at Jansen.

"Just because I won't marry you, Jan, doesn't mean I don't want you to stay with me. A piece of paper doesn't mean anything. It's just paper. You wipe your ass with paper when you shit, that's about as worthless as you can get."

"It would mean something to me. It would mean that you and I are committed."

"You're in my bed every night. I've asked you to move in. I love you, my kids love you. That's commitment. Besides there's no reason to buy the cow—"

"I swear on all that's holy if you tell me one more time about the milk being free, I may strangle you."

"Well? It's true! And that doesn't have anything to do with commitment either."

"Jesus, maybe I should be committed for loving you," he mutters.

"Some love," I huff, turning back around to look at the tack.

"What's that supposed to mean?"

"How do you love someone and walk away from them? My whole life that's what happened. Someone professes to love me, and then, when I need them the most, they just walk away. How is that love, Jan?"

"Ida Sue—"

"Even my parents. They're supposed to love and protect their child. That's stronger than even a marriage certificate in your eyes, right? My parents didn't know the meaning of protection and their love was as brittle as the fucking wind. They left me vulnerable. They made it easy for a predator to find me, to take everything away from me in one single act of violence and just when I needed them most? They couldn't even try to believe me. They kicked me out to live in the streets."

"Ida Sue, Darlin'…"

"No. You don't get to feel pity for me, Jan. I am not someone to be pitied. I'm strong and I'll make sure my kids are strong. I don't need anyone's pity!"

"I've had that message clear for a long time now, Ida Sue. Trust me, I get it. You don't need anyone," he says, turning away from me.

"That's where you're wrong, Jan," I state brokenly, laying it all out. I slide to the floor and let the wall hold my back.

"Ida—"

"I needed you and you're walking away, just like all the others."

53

Jansen

"I'M NOT LEAVING, Ida Sue. You're pushing me away. You've got in your head that everyone left you, but Orville didn't, right? He gave you beautiful babies and a ranch that will take care of you the rest of your life."

"He left, too."

"He died, Darlin', there's not much you can do to stop the sands from moving through that hourglass. When it's your time, it's just your time."

"I guess," she says, her voice sounding unbelievably sad.

"Ida Sue, can you try to see this from my point of view? I don't have one thing to offer you that you need. Nothing. I feel like there's not one reason for me to be here. I was trying, because you needed me to take care of the ranch, but you don't need that anymore. I can't stay here, sleeping with the woman I love, but not having any claim to anything or anyone."

"You want me to put your name on the deed? Because if that's it, Jansen, I'll do it——"

"Fuck, no. I don't want your ranch, Ida Sue. This is land you got from your late husband. It's hard enough sleeping in the bed you used to share with him."

"Is that what all this is about? Your pride is hurt because your hotdog is sliding into a used bun?"

I shake my head. I don't know if I'll ever get used to this woman.

"Can you never use hotdogs and buns as an example when we talk about me making love to you again?"

"That should be easy enough, since you're leaving."

"How is it so easy for you to put my name on a deed to land that you're getting an obscene amount of money from and not marry me? I don't understand."

"Every time I try to reach for happiness it disappears, Jan. *Every single time.*"

"Ida Sue—"

"You're not sharing the bed I had with Orville. Orville and I didn't share a bed."

I don't know what to say to that, so I let it go and just wait. My feet walk to her corner though, without thought and I find myself sliding down the wall to sit beside her. My hand reaches over to capture one of hers and our fingers twine together and rest on my leg. Then, I just let her talk.

"We had sex. In his bedroom, which is Maggie's room now."

"I don't really need to hear—"

"I loved Orville and he loved me, but it wasn't... it's not..." She sighs, seemingly unable to find the words. I just stay quiet and wait, knowing she needs to get it out and also because I need to hear it.

"He was lonely. I needed someone to save me from drowning, and I was drowning, Jan. Some days, since his death, I feel like I still am. I hate admitting that. I hate that I feel weak. I can't be weak. I have nine kids and none of them asked to be here, I brought them into this world and I'm glad. My children are beautiful, smart, loving and these complicated individuals that deserve all the good in the world. They're the reason I keep getting out of bed every morning."

"Ida Sue, you're about the farthest thing from weak as I've ever seen in my life."

"Jan—"

I reach over and cup the side of her face, turning her so she's looking at me.

"Honey Girl, you're so strong you're a freaking force of nature."

"Don't leave me, Jan. I'm begging you to stay. How is that for strong?"

"Will you marry me?"

"Jan—"

"Not now, Ida Sue. But in the future, once I've proved to whatever demon lives in that head of yours that I'm here to stay, will you finally marry me?"

"Someday, maybe. But you do know that Texas is a common law state. Technically, if you stick around we will be married."

"You're stubborn, Ida Sue."

"I've been told that before," she says with her first hint of a smile. "Actually, I think you said that just a little bit ago," she adds, her grin deepening.

"I'm not going to stop asking you, common law or not, Darlin'."

"I guess I can deal with that," she murmurs.

"It's going to be hard working in Lawson and coming back here every night. But I reckon' we'll muddle through."

"Why would you work in Lawson?"

"That's where the job is Ida Sue."

"You have a job here."

"Darlin' I can't keep working here. I haven't even cashed the last two checks you paid me. I'm not going to sleep with the woman who is signing my checks. It feels too much like you're paying me for services rendered in the bedroom."

"Bullshit. Besides if I was doing that, then I'm severely underpaying you."

I laugh and it's the first time I feel like I've laughed in weeks.

"Except for lately, you've been slacking on the job," she says with a grin.

"You're insane, Darlin'. Damn good for my ego, but definitely crazy."

"That's okay, it will just keep you on your toes."

"I got to admit, I do like that."

Ida Sue moves then, straddling my lap and sitting down on it so that we're facing. It seems unreal that after the emotional talk we've just had that something that simple could make my cock go instantly hard, but I do, my dick immediately pushing against my jeans to connect with her heat that I can feel even through our clothes.

"Then, I'm going to make a promise to you, Cowboy."

"What's that?" I ask, my arms going around her.

"I'm going to make it my mission to keep you on your toes for the rest of our lives."

"Is that a fact?"

"Definitely."

"That sounds awfully permanent, Ida Sue."

"Jan, it's taken me thirty-eight years to find love. If you think I'm going to give it up now, you're the one who's crazy."

"Give me your lips, Honey Girl."

"Always, Jan. Always," she whispers as she bends down to press her lips to mine and I let go of the last little bit of doubt I have.

54

Jansen

"TAKE YOUR CLOTHES OFF, DARLIN'."

She stands up after our kiss, our gazes locked together. I stand to face her, already taking my clothes off. We do it together. I take my shirt off, she takes hers off with a smile that I know I'll remember for the rest of my life. She kicks off her shoes, I pull off my socks. It's like some kind of partner strip-tease, but much sexier from my view, I'm sure.

"Did I ever tell you that I love the fact you go commando, Jansen Reed?"

"Now is not the time to be cute, Ida Sue."

"It's not?"

"No, you're distracting me."

"Jansen, I—"

"You're going to turn around and put your hands on the wall, Honey Girl."

I see the surprise on her face, but her gaze drops down and watches as I stroke my hard cock. She rubs her lips together, moistening them and her gaze slowly travels back up to my face.

"This is me... turning around like a good girl," she whispers. I grin. She can't help herself. I close the distance between us and she looks over her shoulder as if to dare me.

"I love your body, Darlin'," I murmur against her skin as I gather her hair in my hands pulling it to one side and draping it over her shoulder. "The way it looks, the way it tastes…"

As I'm talking I kiss along the curve of her neck, along the line of her clavicle, and slowly meander down her back. I let my tongue trail an imaginary path, tasting her. I stop mid-back and let my hand snake around to hold her soft breasts, squeezing them.

"Jan," she whispers, her head going back in pleasure, her pert nipples pushing against the palms of my hands.

"I really love the way it feels," I add.

I squeeze harder, before letting my hands drop down so the pads of my fingers can dance over her ribs, feel the flesh that has risen into small bumps that have skated over her skin with her excitement. Her breathing is coming faster now and I can hear the anticipation in it. I love that my touch does this to her.

That I do this to her.

Me… and only me.

My hands glide to her hips as I crouch down and continue kissing her back. Before the night is over, I'm going to kiss every inch of Ida Sue.

Every. Fucking. Inch.

I stop at the small of her back, my hands moving to her thighs, holding her in place, refusing to allow her move, even though her body is restless.

She tries to fight me, needing more. I don't give her what she wants. I'm in control here and she won't be able to do anything but submit… *and let go.*

"Jan, please."

Ida Sue's voice is broken, threaded with hunger, but is as soft as a summer breeze. There's something about it that calls me— will always call me. She's my place, my shelter, my home. I was a fool to think I could have ever given her up. I would have come back. I'd always come back for her.

"I really love your ass, Darlin'," I murmur, kissing one of the silky white globes while squeezing it with my hand.

I do the other one the same, too—just so it won't feel left out and I can feel her trembling. Her hips are rocking in a disjointed movement as her hips thrust into nothing but air. I can smell her excitement and I let my fingers move slowly between the cleft of her ass—which only makes her shuddering intensify—especially as I press against the entrance of her ass.

"Please, Jan," she begs, widening her stance, her hands slapping against the wall, her ass thrusting out against my face.

I bite the juicy, apple-shaped globe, not even trying to be gentle and she moans a sound that makes my leaking dick jerk with hunger, as one long line of pre-cum drips from the head and glides along my shaft, all the way to my balls, which are aching with the need to fill her with cum.

My fingers follow the curves of her body and seek out the entrance of her sweet pussy, tunneling into the wet depths so urgently, it's almost harsh. Her walls clamp down against my digits as I fuck her, moving them in and out of her quickly— staying just long enough to tease her, but not enough to make her come.

She tries to find a rhythm, but I don't give that to her. She's not going to come on my hand. She's going to come on my dick, come apart while I paint the inside of her with my cum, branding her with it.

"Damn it, Jan, give it to me," she growls, her voice smoky and desperate.

As my fingers slide out of her tight little cunt I widen them and push up seeking out her clit. It's swollen and throbbing almost as much as the head of my cock. I capture it and then scissor across it, feeling her sweet juices gush against my skin. I want to bury my head between her legs and drink her down, but that's not how this round is going to go.

I have to be inside of her and I have to be inside of her now.

I don't even have the energy to stand back up and slam into her. I'm too desperate to get inside her wet heat. I'm aching way too much for that, dying to have her.

I go to the floor, sitting down and positioning myself under her. From this position I can see the way her juices are descending from her pussy and dripping along the inside of her thighs, coating them. Again, if I wasn't so desperate to get inside of her, I'd bury my face right there, thrust my tongue inside of her and eat her out while she comes all over me.

I'll definitely do that later, but for now I reach up and my hands grab each of her hips, with bruising force.

"On your knees, Ida Sue. *Now.*"

I order her, my voice barely recognizable now. It's hoarse and filled with a savage hunger—my need for her that strong.

Immediately her body goes limp. She tries to face me, but I don't let her. I want her riding my cock just like this.

Just like fucking this.

"Jan," she cries out as desperate as I am.

"Reach down and guide me into you, Darlin'. Bring me home."

I don't know if she understands the significance of what I'm saying, but I do. Years and years of wandering around and feeling lost are gone now.

Completely gone.

That's a fucking feeling that I can't enjoy now, I'm too far gone. As her hand wraps around my throbbing cock, this time my head goes back as a blast of pleasure so intense it robs me of breath, shoots through my body. She squeezes me, my head rubbing against her pulsing clit and sliding in her juices before finding entrance and sliding into her tight cunt.

"Fuck," she hisses. My cock is thick and wide, but right now I don't think I've ever been this hard and I've gone in at an angle, pushing against her inner walls.

My eyes close as she takes me all the way in, my balls press against her wet entrance.

"Ride me, Darlin'. Ride your man."

My voice is a growl as my hands capture her hips and I move her up and down on my cock, helping her find the pace she needs. I watch our bodies move for as long as I can, watch as she moves up and down on my shaft, my cock glistening with her desire, watching as inch by inch of my thick cock disappears into her body and then slides back out. It's fucking beautiful. Our pace fierce, our fucking violent as she bounces and rides, taking every damn thing she needs from me. I could take in this show for days, fuck her just like this—endlessly. But, all too soon, I feel electricity fire through me, my balls harden, hurt with the load of cum I have to give her. Heat spreads through me and I know I can't hold back much longer.

My hands snake up to grab her breasts as I pull—no, I slam her down on my cock—as I roughly yank and pinch her nipples, my hands overflowing with her tits. She grinds her sweet little pussy against me, using my body to take her exactly where she needs to go. Her head goes back, her hair falling against me like a damn curtain. I squeeze her tits harder, my body thrusting and grinding too, fucking her so hard that a fine sheen of sweat is covering our bodies, the room smelling like dirty, rough sex and I fucking love every minute of it.

"Jan... I... I need to come, baby."

I let go of one breast, to move my hand down her stomach to find her pussy. I can't see the path I'm making, but I'm a creature of instinct now, knowing exactly where I'm going and only wanting to bring my woman pleasure—to make her cum as I unload inside of her.

I seek and find her clit and I rub against it, torture it, scrape, and then eventually massage it as she drowns my fingers in her cum and I feel her orgasm release and overtake her body.

"Jan...." It's a moan, but it's my name and it's filled with pleasure as she comes, bathing my shaft and her sweet pussy sucks my cock so tight, fisting it so tight that I can't remember to breathe and that's when I give it to her.

I come so hard that for a second, I wonder if I won't lose consciousness. I give her everything I have and without thought I bite into her shoulder as I do it, marking her on the outside as clearly as I'm marking her on the inside.

55

Jansen

SIX MONTHS LATER

"JAN? THAT YOU?"

"Who in the hell else would be crawling in your bed at this time of night, Lovey?" I grumble.

I stripped before I got in and now I pull her warm body back into mine and close my eyes at the sensations that hit me. Never has coming home been this fucking sweet. I'm not even sure I had a home before now.

"Don't get grumpy. I missed you," she murmurs, snuggling that sexy little ass against me and kissing the arm I have wrapped around, holding her breasts.

"Sorry, Darlin', it was just a long ride home," I tell her, kissing the top of her head. "Go back to sleep."

"You expect me to go to sleep with that steel rod poking me in the ass?" she giggles.

"He'll settle down in a bit, he's just happy to see you," I smile into her hair, feeling the stress from the day beginning to ease away.

"What time is it?"

"One a.m."

"Jan, Sweetheart, I've held my tongue on this job of yours, but I'm done."

"Ida Sue, I told you——"

I stop talking when she flops over on her back and looks at me.

"Don't start, Jansen Reed. You drive two hours to get to work, work your ass to the bone all day, drive two hours back and then check on everything here before you can get in our bed. The kids miss you and Mary's forgetting who you are, because you're never here."

"I know, Darlin'. I'm trying to look in Mason for jobs, but the sad truth is there just aren't that many right now.

"I know, which is why I did this," she mumbles and she turns to her side and opens up her nightstand drawer, then after getting some papers out of it, turns back to me. "Here."

I frown looking at the papers she gave me, sigh and then sit up, leaning back against the headboard. I flip on the bedside lamp and read what she has.

"You bought the farm next door?"

"Not exactly. If I had bought it, those loan papers attached wouldn't be there. But, because I'm on my way to being common law married to a pig-headed, stubborn as a mule, man, I took *your* money and put a down payment on the farm next door and financed the rest for umpteen years."

"My money?" I'm still not understanding what she did, the how or the why.

"Money you used to pay up all the back payments, interest and junk, getting the ranch out of foreclosure."

"Ida Sue, damn it!"

"Jansen Reed, damn it! You saved my ass with *your* money and yet when it comes to helping you and saving your ass from ending up in an early grave, all because you're killing yourself working and traveling, you bitch. You do realize what a double standard that is, right?"

"This down payment is more than I paid to catch the ranch up," I grumble, finally looking at the papers.

"I added in the month of paychecks you wouldn't cash."

"Christ."

"So, now you own more land. I fail to see how—"

"No, *you* own land. Look at the name of the farm, Cowboy."

"Reed Farm?"

"Completely yours, along with the payments, unfortunately."

"Ida Sue, what in the hell am I going to do with a farm?"

"Turn it into a horse ranch, fence it in with what we have now and run cows, hell do nothing but plant watermelons. I don't really care. But, whatever you do, we'll live off that income and what the oil brings in I'll put back for the kids and…."

"Ida Sue, this is…"

"Jansen, I've had happy things happen to me—nine to be exact—but, before you I never felt truly secure and happy."

"Honey…" I murmur, not knowing exactly what to say to that.

"I find the happier I get… the more I'm apt to…."

"Want sex? Because I got to tell you, Darlin', you can wear a man out on a good day, but the last three months…." I let out a long whistle to make my point.

"Are you complaining?"

"Hell, no. Just wondering if I should check into vitamins so I can keep up," I wink.

"I've been reading on that, we need a peach grove and definitely a watermelon patch—hence the suggestion, and..."

"Should I ask why?"

"I'll explain later, anyways as I was explaining that we'll use the oil money for the kids and for when I need to soothe my soul. Honestly, the happier I get the more I seem to get a wild hair..."

"What exactly is a wild hair?" I laugh.

"Well, remember last month when I decided to buy Jules's shop out from under her because she just annoyed me to no end?"

"Yeah, I remember. I thought it was kind of poetic justice that you turned it into a feed store called Pig Wallers."

"Well, she really is a pig and she does waller in the mud and like to sling it around. I thought it was nice of me to name it after her, really. I'm not sure Jules thought so—especially after I sold the shop for a dollar to the Reverend's soon to be ex-wife."

"I love you, crazy woman," I laugh, bending down to kiss her.

Eventually we break apart and she rests her head on my chest, her fingers lazily moving through the hair there.

"Anyways, I'm just saying that I may from time to time, buy things just because I can make my kids happy, or make sure my friends find happiness… or you…. That's okay, right?"

"That's more than okay, Ida Sue."

"So, it's settled? You'll fix up Reed Farms for us and we'll save this place for the kids and—"

"Not quite," I sigh and she looks up at me.

"I'm a stubborn old cuss, but I finally realized something just now."

"What's that?"

"I've never been truly happy until you came into my life either, Ida Sue. You need to know that."

"We were made for each other."

"That we were. So, I'm done fighting it."

"You were fighting being in love with me?" she asks, raising an eyebrow at the question, clearly not happy with that thought.

"I was fighting the fact that you had all this money and didn't really need me."

"That's just being dumber than a bucket of rocks, Jan."

"You're always such a sweet talker," I laugh.

"I mean it. I'd give up all of the money if it meant keeping you, Jansen Reed."

"You really mean that," I respond and it's a statement not a question.

"Jansen, I've spent my life only being half alive before you came along. I love you."

"And I love you…so…"

"Yeah?"

"We'll join Reed Farm with the Lucas Ranch and make it one huge property."

"Oh… We'll be cattle barons?"

"Definitely."

"I like the way you think."

"And we won't worry about dividing up who owns what. You win, Lovey. I finally get it."

"Do you, really?

"I really do. We're not separate. We're a team."

"And we always will be."

"There's only one more thing that would make it perfect, Honey Girl."

"What's that?"

"Will you marry me?"

She rolls her eyes at me and grins. We both know her answer, but it doesn't bother me anymore. She's right. It's just a piece of paper. I have her heart.

She pulls the covers off of us and takes the papers from my hand and puts them on the nightstand. My gaze moves over her naked body as she straddles me and positions herself so that my cock is pressing against her wet heat, and then slides between the lips of her pussy.

"How many times do I have to tell you, Cowboy that you don't buy the cow if the milk is free?" she asks, and then she reaches down and guides my cock inside of her. My head goes back in pleasure as my gaze locks with hers.

"I love you, Ida Sue.

"I love you, Jansen," she answers, and then slowly begins riding me, bringing us both into heaven.

I don't know how I got so damn lucky in life, but now that I have Ida Sue and these crazy kids in my life, I realize that I'm right where I belong.

I'm home.

Ida Sue is what I was searching for my whole life.

I wish I could have met her sooner, loved her longer, but it worked out the way it was supposed to. She was meant to be a mother to those nine kids, who are so much like her that it is scary. I was meant to come into their lives when I did. I may not have been Ida Sue's first kiss, or hell, even the first time she felt love. But, I'm damned sure her last, because I'm not a fool. I have her heart…

And I'm never letting her go.

Epilogue One

JANSEN

Five Years Later

"Are you ready, Maggie love?" I ask my beautiful girl. She might not be mine by blood, but these last five years have just made these kids and Ida Sue mine in every way that matters.

"I'm scared, Jansen," she admits quietly.

"You don't have to do this, Maggie. You know that, right? Your Momma and I are right here for you to lean on. There's no reason for you to go through with this marriage."

"I'm pregnant, Jansen. My child deserves to grow up with both of his or her parents in the same home," she says and it's an old argument. Ida Sue and I both have tried to talk her out of this marriage, but we haven't gotten anywhere. If there's one thing I know about the Lucas women it's that they're headstrong and independent.

"That baby deserves to have a mommy that's happy. That's all that matters, little one. If you're not happy there's no way the baby is going to be."

"Bryant will be good to me and the baby. He loves us," she says and I have to wonder if she's trying to convince herself more than she is me.

"You're only twenty-one——"

"Mom had me by that age, and had White and Gray. She was a great mom and I'm going to be too, Jansen. I swear I will be."

"You'll be an amazing momma, Maggie May, but you don't have to be married to be that mom."

"You sound like my mother," she laughs.

"I never told you, not once since you came to the ranch, Jansen."

"What's that, Sweetheart?"

"I had one man I thought of as my dad, but God blessed me with a second one when he brought you into my life."

Emotion chokes me up and I'm not ashamed one damn bit that tears fall from my eyes.

"I never told any of you, either, that I may not have been able to father kids, but if I had, I would have wanted them to be just like you. I wouldn't have changed a thing. I love you like you were mine, Maggie—all of you. Never doubt that, Magnolia Tree Marie Lucas."

"Ew, Jansen, you didn't have to use my full name," she laughs through her tears as I hug her, holding her close, if only for another couple of minutes.

"Well, okay, maybe I would have changed your names slightly," I laugh, giving her one final squeeze.

"If only," she says, laying her head on my shoulder.

Outside in the yard I can hear the bridal music begin to play.

"There's still time, Maggie," I murmur in her ear.

"I'm ready," she answers and my heart hurts. She's not ready, and not because she won't make some man a great wife. It's because the man she picked won't make her a good husband, but her mother and I have both tried to get her to see that. The thing I'm learning most with kids is that you can love them, but when it comes down to it, you have to let them make their own mistakes. All you can do is be around to cushion the blow when they fall.

"Then we better get going," I murmur kissing the top of her head one more time, wishing I could do more than just watch her make a mistake...

"You okay, Lovey?"

It's after the wedding. And Ida Sue and I are out on the front porch in the swing, looking at the stars. All the guests have left. Blue is still suffering from a bad breakup with Meadow and Cyan is mooning over some girl at school, so they went off together—God only knows what they are up to. Cyan is wild as a mink and Blue has the same streak, he's just quieter about it. Green and his fiancé, Marissa took Petal with them to the movies, and Black... I have no idea what girl he's out with this week, and sweet little Mary is out like a light.

All of that means the house is quiet and my woman and I should be making the most of it all... but, she's been quiet since Maggie and Bryant drove off with the just married sign hanging off the bumper of their car.

"She's making a mistake, Jan."

"She probably is."

"He's going to hurt my baby..."

"He probably is."

"Will you stop being so calm!?!?"

"Lovey, what do you want me to do? If you can think of one damn thing I can do to make any of this better, I'll do it. But, she's as headstrong as you are and she wouldn't listen to either one of us."

"I know," she finally sighs, falling back into me.

"I love you, Honey Girl."

"I love you, too, Jan."

I reach down in my pocket and pull out the ring box that I've kept close the last five years.

"You going to marry me yet, Lovey?"

"In Texas, technically we're already married," she murmurs, closing the lid on the box.

"You're a hard woman," I laugh, I already knew her answer, but it doesn't bother me anymore. This is who she is, and eventually she'll know that I'm not going anywhere.

"Haven't you heard that old saying about, not rocking the boat? Besides, I've told you and told you a million times over—"

"Ida Sue, don't say it."

"But it's true. There's no need to buy the cow, when you're already getting the milk for free."

I stand up, putting the ring back in my pocket. I'll ask her when one of the kids get married again. Might as well make it a tradition. I bend down and scoop Ida Sue in my arms. She squeals and wraps her arms around me.

"What are you doing?"

"I figure if we're going to live in sin, we might as well get to sinning."

"I do like the sound of that, but we'll have to be quiet. Mary is sleeping."

"Grab that monitor," I order her, leaning down so she can.

Ida Sue still keeps a monitor in Mary's room, because she's been sleepwalking.

"What's in that deliciously wicked mind of yours, Cowboy?"

"We haven't worshipped each other's bodies in the old playhouse in a while. There's a table in it. It might not be our table, but it is solid…" I tell her with a wink.

"Worshipped?" she giggles.

"Every time with you, Ida Sue, is close to a religious experience." I smirk as I open the door and let us inside.

Once there, I let her slide to the floor, she puts the monitor down on the floor and I lock the door on the playhouse.

"I guess it's my job to take you to church then, Jan," she says pulling her shirt off.

"I like the way you think, Honey Girl."

"You'll like it even more when you see what I do when I get on my knees and give thanks…"

Right After Green's Wedding to Marissa

"God, I'm glad that's over," Maggie says, collapsing on the swing. I sit down beside her with a heartfelt sigh.

"Me too," I answer, as sad about the wedding we just attended as Maggie is.

Maggie's back home now. Her marriage to Bryant didn't even last a year. They lost their child and that loss drove a wedge between them. I have to say, I was wrong about Bryant and I was sad to see Maggie move back home, but she worked hard toward her degree. I'm proud of her.

Green, on the other hand I want to ring his neck.

"I don't remember Marissa being such a bitch while her and Green were dating," Black mutters.

"That's because she wasn't," Cyan says, undoing his tie.

"Maybe it's pregnancy hormones," Blue adds in.

"Maybe it's just because of the wedding and she'll be better now?" Maggie says, but none of us really believe that.

The Marissa we saw today is nothing like the one we've gotten to know. It's like a light switch went off and she changed completely. My boy is miserable. He only started dating Marissa when Cynthia broke his heart. At this point I wouldn't give a hill of beans for either girl. I'm thinking my boy's picker is broken. Either that, or he's letting the wrong head do his thinking.

Whatever it is, it's hurting him. I can see it in his eyes, but he's got a baby coming and he's bound and determined to give that child everything he can—even if it means tying himself to a woman who makes more demands than the Queen of England.

"She knows she's got Green hogtied and now that he's locked up, she's letting it all hang out," Jansen grumbles.

"Jan—"

"On this, I'm speaking from experience, Lovey," he says and from the conversations we've had about his ex-wife, I can't argue with him. If I ever meet her, I'm going to throat punch her, maybe kick her a few times just for fun and eventually thank her for being a complete idiot and letting Jansen get away.

"This is my fault," I say with a sigh.

"How do you figure? Did you tell Green to do the mattress mambo without a raincoat?" Jansen asks.

"No, but instead of teaching them to work hard and always be a family, maybe I should have taught them to keep it in their pants," I mutter.

"Or to keep their pants on," Black adds, wiggling his eyebrows at Maggie.

"I'm going to go inside and check on Mary and Petal," Maggie says, her voice sad. She walks in the house, the screen door slamming behind her.

"Smooth, Black. Real smooth, you douche," Blue growls, elbowing his brother a little too hard.

"Shit, I wasn't thinking. I'll go make sure she's okay," he says and moves inside.

I just sigh. I'm feeling kind of defeated. I can't seem to make sure any of my kids are happy. Damn it, that has to stop. If the next child of mine to walk down the aisle isn't completely happy, I'm going to start making sure they get matched up with someone I know will make them happy—because it's clear they can't be trusted to decide on their own.

They deserve to find someone like my Jan. I stand up and go over and kiss him, just needing that contact.

"What was that for?" he asks, his hand sliding against the inside of my throat and his thumb brushing up against my cheek.

"I'm just incredibly thankful for you, Cowboy."

"Ew gross. Can't you guys take it to the playhouse?" Cyan mutters.

"What do you know about the playhouse?" Jansen asks as I giggle.

"Oh please, everyone knows what you two do in that playhouse. Haven't you noticed how we all avoid it like the plague?"

"We're just having a little meeting with the Lord. Ain't that right, Jan?"

"Amen," he says with a naughty wink.

"Hey Blue?"

"Yeah, Jan?"

"Back my truck close to the porch, will you?"

"You better not kill my grass, Jansen Reed," I warn him as Black grabs Jansen's keys and goes running to the driveway. "If you do, there won't be enough altar calls to save you."

"Your grass is safe, Lovey. I have a surprise for you."

"What kind of surprise?" I ask, eyeing him skeptically.

"First things first," he says and he gets down on one knee.

Crap.

"Ida Sue Lucas? Will you marry me?" he asks, holding our ring up.

He asks often, so often I now think of the ring as "ours" even if I have never agreed to wear it. Sometimes I think he just asks to annoy me. Sometimes I want to say yes, but things are so wonderful, I'm scared to. If I say yes that's like waving a red flag at fate and telling them to come fuck with me, and I don't want that.

"Jansen, I told you we're already married according to Texas law," I mumble lamely.

"Yes or no, Ida Sue."

"No," I tell him gently. "I already told you there's no point in buying the cow if the milk is free."

"Gross, Mom!" Cyan yells.

"The last thing I want to think about is my mom's *milk*," Black mutters, coming back out of the house.

"You didn't complain when I was breast feeding you. Hell, you hung on to the titty more than any other kid I had. I think you were like four. Probably would have kept going, but I refused. You kept trying to bite my nipple off."

I'm lying of course, Black was eight months, but I'm enjoying the way he's turning green and looking sick.

"Excuse me while I go throw up now," Black growls.

"You left me with no other choice, Ida Sue," Jansen says, getting my attention again.

"What does that mean?" I ask, scared he might try to leave again. I won't let him. He's stuck with me if I have to tie him to my bed until he sees things my way…. That's actually *not* a bad idea… I might try that tonight.

Blue finishes backing the truck up and I frown as Jansen stands and goes and lets his tailgate down.

"What's that?" I ask, motioning to the huge cage in the back with an old blue sheet draped over it

"That's your surprise," Jansen says, yanking the sheet off.

My breath catches as I look at the prettiest little calf I've ever seen. It's solid white, except its hooves, ears and nose. Those are all black as coal. The top of its head is a mixture of both colors.

"Jansen, its beautiful. Is this one of ours?"

"Hell no, it's too scrawny for that. She's a different breed than what we run. I bought her today off of an old friend," he says, and that makes sense, because I doubt this little girl would weigh more than sixty pounds.

"You bought her?" I ask, now standing beside him, petting the baby calf and admiring how soft its hair is.

"I did, which brings me to the rest of your present," he says reaching into the bed of the truck to pull out a big starter bottle with an even bigger nipple on it.

"Damn don't show that to Black, he'll steal it," Cyan laughs and Black shoves him. I take the bottle and run my finger over the teat, looking at Jansen confused.

"The mommy died. My buddy didn't have a replacement cow to feed it, and wasn't about to handfeed the little booger. So, it's now your responsibility."

"You bought me…." I trail off, confused.

"I bought the damn cow, Ida Sue and let me tell you something the milk in that bottle is definitely not free."

It takes me a minute, but when it hits me I throw my head back and laugh.

"God, I love you," I tell him, when my laughter finally dies down enough so I can talk.

Jansen wraps me up in his arms and kisses me quickly on the lips.

"And I love you, Honey Girl. I'll always love you," he vows and I know he means it, because Jansen never says anything that he doesn't mean.

I look at my new pet cow. I have plans for that little thing. I'll have the only cow around that thinks he's a dog. I wonder if I can train him to fetch? I bet I can. He's smart, you can see it in his eyes. Maybe I'll even teach him to fetch Jan's slippers at night. Of course, Jan doesn't wear slippers, but I'll pout until he starts.

After all, I have to keep him on his toes. I promised him that years ago and it's a promise I intend on keeping…

For the rest of our lives.

The End.

Read More Jordan
WITH THESE TITLES:

Lucas Brothers Series

Perfect Stroke
Raging Heart On
Happy Trail
Cocked & Loaded

Doing Bad Things Series

Going Down Hard
In Too Deep
Taking It Slow

Savage Brothers MC—Tennessee Chapter

Devil
Diesel
Rory

Savage Brothers MC

Breaking Dragon
Saving Dancer
Loving Nicole
Claiming Crusher
Trusting Bull
Needing Carrie

Devil's Blaze MC

Captured
Burned
Released
Shafted
Beast
Beauty

Pen Name Baylee Rose & Re-released
Filthy Florida Alphas Series

Unlawful Seizure
Unjustified Demands
Unwritten Rules

Links:

Here's my social media links! Make sure you sign up for my newsletter. I give things away there and you get to see things before others! I also have a blog on my webpage you can subscribe to and besides my strange ramblings I'll update you on my work in progress.

Newsletter Subscription
  Facebook Reading Group
  Facebook Page
  Twitter
  Webpage
  Bookbub
  Instagram

Text Alerts (US Subscribers Only—Standard Text Messaging Rates May Apply):
  Text *JORDAN* to 797979 to be the first to know when Jordan has a sale or released a new book.